He didn't *look* passionate——

Meeting the consultant's gaze was like being unexpectedly ducked in an Arctic stream, and Carrie decided that no passion lurked behind *that* glacial exterior. And, glancing around in surprise, she saw that even Mr Cunningham had departed, leaving her alone with the boss.

Feeling suddenly nervous, she fiddled with the case-notes in front of her, as Robert Sheraton lounged in the comfortable armchair opposite. If she put out her hand, she could touch him, and the thought was frightening in a delicious sort of way.

Dear Reader

Welcome to Medical Romances! This month sees the innovation of an editor letter, which we hope you will find interesting and informative.

We welcome back Betty Beaty after a long absence from the list, and launch Margaret Holt with her first book, as well as offering Kathleen Farrell and Hazel Fisher—happy reading!

The Editor

Hazel Fisher was a late entrant into nursing and was briefly a general nursing student before deciding on psychiatry. She worked as a mental nurse for several years before writing full-time.

Having lived in East Sussex all her life, she admits that most of her plots come when she's doing the household chores! She enjoys writing medical romances as they provide much needed escapism—for her as well as the readers!

Recent titles by the same author:

LUCY'S CHALLENGE
A DREAM WORTH SHARING

CAROLINE'S CONQUEST

BY

HAZEL FISHER

MILLS & BOON LIMITED
ETON HOUSE   18–24 PARADISE ROAD
RICHMOND   SURREY   TW9 1SR

First published in Great Britain 1992
by Mills & Boon Limited

© Hazel Fisher 1992

Australian copyright 1992
Philippine copyright 1992
This edition 1992

ISBN 0 263 77659 X

Set in 10 on 10½ pt Linotron Plantin
03-9205-62141

Typeset in Great Britain by Centracet, Cambridge
Made and printed in Great Britain

CHAPTER ONE

'ARE you sure this is the right road?' Nurse Caroline West asked for the umpteenth time, and Phil Mackie growled,

'If you ask me that just once more, Carrie, I'll stop and dump you by the roadside!'

Since Phil was known for his equable temperament, this seemed unlikely, but Carrie obligingly shut up, feeling at the same time that they *were* on the wrong road. They should have turned left instead of right at the small, unlit country crossroads a couple of miles back, but as Phil had reached the dizzy heights of houseman he presumably knew what he was doing. If she was late on duty just once more, though. . . The tall, spare figure of her tutor loomed large in Carrie's imagination, and she hurriedly turned her mind to something else.

The main topic of conversation among the St Hilda's learners at the moment was what the new consultant gynaecologist would be like, since rumour had it that he was one of the 'little tin god' breed who did not condescend to notice any nurse below the rank of nursing officer. This rumour was of interest to Carrie, who was to begin her gynae experience after Christmas. Her temper rose—she certainly wasn't going to bow and scrape before him no matter *how* proud and arrogant he was! She nibbled her full lower lip, memory of another time, another surgeon coming back to her, then she shrugged it aside, just as Phil's ancient car shuddered then stopped dead.

She opened her mouth in dismay, but Phil forestalled her. 'Don't nag, Carrie!' His voice was sharp, and Carrie began to shake her head.

'I wasn't going to, really! Haven't run out of petrol, have you?' she asked suspiciously, well aware that Phil

5

had something of a reputation, though surely, after the firmness with which she had said 'no' last time, he would have got the message.

'According to the petrol gauge, *yes*! I knew I was getting low but I should have had enough to last—it's all your fault!' he charged, turning to Carrie, whose big green eyes grew bigger and rounder with indignation.

'What did *I* do? I still think we're on the wrong road and all I said was——'

'Shut up and get out, there's a good girl.'

Carrie stared in dismay. 'Oh, Phil, no! You aren't going to make me walk?'

He chuckled, his good humour apparently restored. 'Silly child, of course I'm not! What kind of doctor would I be if I made you walk home in the dark? Though we'll both have to walk. There must be a petrol station around here somewhere.'

If Phil had taken the correct turning, there would have been one about a mile further on, but Carrie decided it was wisest not to mention that. It was obvious that he didn't know exactly where they were. If only they hadn't taken that detour to visit one of Phil's friends who seemed to live in the middle of a ten-acre field, and who wasn't at home, anyway. Whatever happened, there was a long chilly walk ahead of them. *And* she was due on night duty at nine o'clock!

In summer, the walk along winding Sussex lanes would have been a pleasant one, but in the middle of a particularly cold December it lacked a certain something, Carrie thought morosely as, hand in hand, she and Phil strode out. Surely they might meet another motorist, even if there wasn't a petrol station?

Unfortunately, there were no Good Samaritans abroad that evening, and the few cars that passed them on the narrow road didn't even slow down, let alone stop. Indeed, Carrie rather felt they accelerated, despite Phil's holding his petrol can aloft.

'If I was in uniform and you were wearing your white

coat they would have stopped,' Carrie muttered as her tired legs at last gave way and she came to a halt, puffing. 'I'm sorry, Phil, but your legs are much longer than mine! You go on and I'll trail behind,' she suggested, and although Phil protested it was only a mild protest. Then he shook his head.

'No, of course you can't! What am I thinking of? The next car that passes probably *will* stop if the driver sees a lone girl. You ought to have stayed in the car, but—you could hide in a hedge, I suppose?' he went on doubtfully, and Carrie shivered.

'I'll do no such thing! You lope on ahead and I'll try to keep within earshot—go on, then!' She urged Phil on, and soon he was lost in the darkness ahead. If only she'd had her sleep after duty last night! But with the chilly interview with the senior tutor, then her friend Ann wanting to cry on her shoulder for some reason, plus loads of tidying up to do after the party, she'd had no more than a couple of cat-naps, not enough to sustain her through another heavy night on Women's Medical. She quickened her pace, despite being nearly asleep on her feet. They must get back in time, they must! She couldn't afford another reprimand. Uncle Charles wasn't best pleased with her as it was and——

She was caught full in the glare from the headlights coming up behind, then they were dipped as, to her consternation, the car slowed. And she was alone! She opened her mouth to call for Phil, then the driver opened the door and peered out, and Carrie tensed, ready to make a run for it if the man was alone.

Then, seeing the woman sitting beside him, Carrie blurted out, 'We've run out of petrol! We left the car back at——'

'Yes, I saw the warning triangle,' the man broke in curtly. Then he glanced ahead to where Phil was just loping into view. 'Hasn't your young man enough sense to stay with you? What would have happened if I'd been one of those kerbside crawlers?' the good Samaritan demanded, his voice dripping ice. 'Anyway, get in the back and I'll find somewhere to turn. There isn't a service station along here.'

'I knew we should have taken the other turning!' Carrie exclaimed, still hesitant about getting into the car until Phil came puffing up. 'We've found a Good Samaritan, Phil!'

The driver snorted. 'You're lucky to have found *anyone* along here! What possessed you to come this way?' This remark, thank goodness, was hurled at Phil, not at her, and Phil waved a hand vaguely.

'I'm sorry, sir, but we thought this *was* the right road,' he explained glibly, and Carrie bit her tongue. There was no point in trying to apportion blame, and she was getting colder by the minute.

They both got into the back of what Carrie recognised as a BMW, then she quickly began to thank the man's so far silent wife, since the Samaritan himself was obviously in a bad mood.

'We'd like to thank you and your husband for giving us a lift,' Carrie said to the back of the carefully coiffured head. 'I hope we haven't held you up?' She beamed at the head, which turned sharply, eyes like laser beams honing in on her and chilling her to the marrow.

The woman, Carrie saw now, was beautiful in a classical Greek statue sort of way, and probably as cold, for she merely nodded, not even giving Carrie the glimmer of a smile, but the Samaritan made a sound which Carrie thought was suspiciously like a laugh, hurriedly stifled. Knowing it couldn't have been she sat back, her eyes closing without her being aware of it, and she slept through the events that followed.

True, once or twice she was aware of vague murmurings, of disjointed voices coming from a vast distance, but she was safe in the arms of Morpheus and wouldn't have woken if Sussex had been struck by another hurricane.

Then a voice spoke to her. Since it seemed to be

resting against her ear, she heard it clearly and struggled
to come round. On waking, her first thought was that
she had slept through the alarm and would be late on
duty again.

'Oh, Phil, I'll be late!' she wailed, then sat up suddenly
and forced her tired eyes to focus. The first thing they
focused on was the face of a stranger—a darkly handsome stranger, at that, and she thought she must still be
dreaming.

Then it all came back. It was the Good Samaritan! But
where was Phil? Wildly, Carrie glanced about her. She
was still in the back of the sumptuous car, but both Phil
and the Samaritan's wife had gone, and the man himself
was gazing thoughtfully at her from the driver's seat.

'Oh, they've gone,' she said blankly, then shook her
head, trying to clear the muzziness from it. If only she
hadn't gone to that party. Then there was the Christmas
shopping with Phil. A stupid thing to do when what she
really needed was at least ten hours of sleep. 'Oh,' she
said again, then smiled at her benefactor. 'I must have
fallen asleep—where's Dr Mackie?'

'*Dr* Mackie?' It was the Samaritan's turn to look blank.
Then a wary expression came to his eyes—eyes which
Carrie saw were as black as his temper. 'He's a doctor?
At St Hilda's?' he asked, and Carrie nodded, then winced
as a pain shot through her head.

'We're both from St Hilda's—he's a houseman on
medical at the moment and I'm a first-year student.
Well, nearly second year, really,' Carrie told him, and
the wary look vanished.

'Ah, he's on medical!' the man murmured, sounding
relieved. 'Well, out you get—this is St Hilda's.' All of a
sudden, the Samaritan became brisk and businesslike,
and before Carrie knew what was happening he had
swung her up in his arms and carried her to a side-door
of the hospital.

Alarmed, she clung to his neck, wondering whether
she was being abducted and ought to scream for help, or

whether she was still in a dream and this wasn't really happening at all. Lack of sleep could do strange things to the brain, hadn't the tutor told her that only this morning? Was it this morning? Or yesterday? Carrie wasn't sure any more. The only thing of which she was sure was that she liked the smell of the Samaritan's aftershave. Then she was dumped unceremoniously on the step and her rescuer stepped back.

'There, this will have to do. I don't know where the nurses' home is, I'm afraid. It isn't far off eight-thirty so you'd better hurry.' With a brisk nod, the tall man strode away before Carrie could ask where he had taken Phil.

Still, if it was nearly time for duty Phil would have to shift for himself; she had more important things to worry about.

They had a death on Ashdown Ward that night and although it was expected Carrie's soft heart still bled for the elderly husband who was left to manage alone.

'The wife—the wife said p-passing away is just like sleep,' Mr Hudson quavered, clutching at Carrie's hand as she sat by him in the visitors' room. 'Do you think that's right, Nurse?'

At twenty, Carrie hadn't given much thought to death. Her own mother had died so long ago that she scarcely remembered her, but she did her best to offer words of comfort now. 'Whatever your own beliefs, Nurse, be sure not to inflict them on to the patients or their relatives.' Those words of her tutor came back to Carrie as she squeezed Mr Hudson's hand.

'That's all it is, Mr Hudson, just a long sleep. A nice rest, away from all the pain,' she added, and he nodded as if satisfied.

'Yes, she's asleep now,' he muttered, seemingly at ease himself, and Carrie stayed with him until the duty doctor arrived to speak to him.

Feeling a good deal more than twenty and longing for

her bed, Carrie went soberly off duty later that morning, watching without envy as the day shift came on, their day-bright faces beaming at her. Only her friend, Ann Haynes, avoided Carrie's eyes as she lagged behind the others.

'Ann? Is something the matter?' Carrie was always quick to offer sympathy to other nurses whose love-lives weren't going smoothly, but with Ann this had never been necessary since she didn't *have* a love-life. And perhaps that was the trouble, Carrie thought shrewdly as Ann at last glanced at her.

'Had a good night, did you? I saw you and—and Phil Mackie in Brighton!'

The way Ann spoke, it sounded almost like an accusation, and Carrie stared at her. 'We were doing some Christmas shopping. Why? Did you want to come? Phil would have given you a lift, I expect—— Oh! Have you seen him this morning? We ran out of petrol last night,' she went on unthinkingly, and Ann gasped, her rather bulbous eyes almost starting from her head.

'Oh, *did* you! A cosy little cuddle in the back seat, was it? How nice for some!' With a sniff, Ann hurried into the ward office, leaving a bewildered Carrie to walk back to the nurses' home, glad she had only one more night to work. One thing was sure, she was going straight to bed!

Dr Phil Mackie spoilt that good resolution, but Carrie was glad to see him. 'Phil! What happened last night?' she whispered fiercely, as they met in the lift going down.

Phil looked vaguely uncomfortable. 'You were all right with that guy, weren't you? I mean, he didn't try anything? I didn't like to leave you, but I wanted to see Bruce about something, and what he said made sense and——'

'*What* guy?' Carrie was more bewildered than ever. 'Oh, the Good Samaritan! I ended up alone in the car with him, if that's what's bothering you!' she added sharply, her round face quivering with indignation. 'And what happened to his wife?'

Before Phil could speak, the lift opened again as another nurse got in. All he had time to say before he got out was, 'He had to drop her off somewhere. Had an appointment or something—see you!'

Then the doors clanged shut and Carrie was on her way down to ground level, her mind in a whirl. So Phil had sent her off to St Hilda's alone with a complete stranger! How dared he?

She burned with indignation, though, if she was honest, and she always tried to be, she had rather enjoyed being swept off her feet and held tightly against a muscular chest! The trouble with knights in shining armour was, she reflected gloomily, that they appeared only in fairy-tales or between the covers of romantic novels; one never met them in real life. Since that particular knight was a married man, perhaps that was just as well!

CHAPTER TWO

MARIGOLD Ward was neat, reasonably tidy, and quiet—the quiet before the storm, Carrie felt. 'There, that's the bedding list finished at last,' she sighed. 'Is the Kardex up-to-date for Mr Sheraton?' She turned to her friend Ann, who had just started on the gynae ward.

'Mm, just doing the last one. I hope he's as late as he said he would be.' Ann glanced up with a smile, a much happier Ann these days. In fact, she had become almost beautiful, Carrie thought without envy. It was surprising what love could do for a girl.

Leaving her friend to tidy the files ready for the consultant's round, Carrie made a quick tour of the ward to see that all was as it should be. Since Sister Carter was at a meeting and the staff nurse was at the dentist's, Carrie was temporarily in charge of Marigold Ward, and was proud that Sister considered her capable enough. Of course, in an emergency she could call on trained nurses from the other wards in the department, but so far everything was going smoothly. Anyway, she was quite capable of taking charge for short periods, though whether Mr Sheraton, the consultant gynaecologist, would think so was another matter. This was his third week in the department but Carrie was still rather in awe of the tall, austere Mr Robert Sheraton, and kept out of his way as much as possible.

Unfortunately, Mr Sheraton was also the Good Samaritan who, just two months before, had literally swept her off her feet! Carrie frowned. It was hardly likely that the man would remember the little nurse he had rescued, yet she had the feeling he *did* remember her and didn't want to acknowledge the fact. His expression had been positively wary when they came face to face on the ward, and even now she sometimes saw his considering gaze on her when he thought himself unobserved. So far, thank goodness, Sister Carter hadn't noticed. *That* would mean a sudden end to Student Nurse Carrie West's career! At the very least, she would be relegated to the sluice and kept there for the duration of Mr Sheraton's rounds.

Carrie put the thought firmly out of her mind, and her eyes softened as she came to Mrs Jordan, who was her favourite patient. Indeed, the bubbly Eileen Jordan was everyone's favourite. She was deep in conversation with her bed neighbour when Carrie approached. They giggled when they saw her, and Carrie wagged a finger at them.,

'Naw, naw, ladies. We can't 'ave you actually *laughin'*. You 'aven't come into 'orspl to enjoy yerselves, you've come to get be'ter,' she said, in a passable imitation of their jovial porter's voice, and the patients chuckled even more.

Eileen Jordan laughed till the tears ran down her thin face. She was a pretty woman of thirty-five who had been admitted for a myomectomy, and was due for discharge any day.

She was a much happier woman now, and Carrie found it difficult to believe that, only a week before, Mrs Jordan had been tense and unhappy, and what Mr Cunningham had described as 'a complete nervous wreck'. Carrie thought that an exaggeration, but certainly the change was remarkable. Mrs Jordan had suffered two spontaneous abortions a while ago, and was still hoping for a child. She had clung nervously to Carrie's hand while the tears flowed, confiding that she was afraid Mr Sheraton would 'take everything out'.

Carrie's gaze softened as she passed by. Yes, she had to admit that was a plus for Robert Sheraton, for he had come in on his day off and sat by Mrs Jordan's bed and just let her talk out her fears. There weren't many surgeons who would do that, so that man had *some* good qualities!

Marigold was arranged in cubicles, and in the next cubicle was a patient who would be going down for a similar operation tomorrow, a 'shelling out' of fibroids. In the gynae suite, nurses, even junior ones, cared for a small group of patients as part of the nursing process, doing everything for that particular group, and this new lady, Mrs Bramley, was one of Carrie's.

'Is everything all right, Mrs Bramley? Mr Sheraton and Mr Cunningham won't be long.' Carrie smiled at her, then decided she could spare a moment to sit down. With a new strain of virus knocking down staff like ninepins, there hadn't been a moment to spare all day.

Doris Bramley sat up in bed, her face pinched and anxious, and Carrie patted her hand. In contrast to Eileen Jordan's hand, Mrs Bramley's was stained with nicotine but was otherwise soft and well-kept.

'Mr Sheraton's kind to patients, so just ask him anything you want,' Carrie continued. 'Oh, did you fill in my form?'

'Yes, I've got it somewhere.' Mrs Bramley rummaged in her locker, then produced a crumpled sheet of A4. 'I've put down everything I could think of, dear.'

Carrie took it and read it quickly. The questionnaire was one her group had devised in consultation with their tutor. It gave the patient a chance to write out her fears, the questions which she might not like to ask the surgeons or might not think of until too late, and it also asked for a patient's-eye view of the op and the condition itself. In many cases the patient didn't know exactly what would be done, or why, and several of the ladies had told Carrie how useful the questionnaire was.

'When I've got a spare minute, I'll check it properly and come and answer your questions—or ask Sister to,' Carrie said, getting up again. Time was marching on. In fact it was positively hurtling along, and it was a good thing Mr Sheraton *was* going to be late. Of course, that

would throw out their routine for the rest of the afternoon and evening and might make them late opening the
doors for visitors, but it couldn't be helped.

She continued her round, assuring the ladies that the
consultant would be with them in about half an hour.
He'd had an emergency operation to perform, and Carrie
hoped fervently that it had gone well, both for the
patient's sake and for the sake of a peaceful ward round.
Mr Sheraton had lost one patient since coming to St
Hilda's and the staff had hardly dared approach him
afterwards. The woman concerned had been a hopeless
case, but he had felt he must attempt to save her life.

Even on good days, Mr Sheraton wasn't an approach-
able man, but when he was in a mood no one was safe
from his acid tongue, not even the patients. Yet they
adored him. Why, Carrie couldn't think. Of course, in a
good mood, he *was* good at answering patients' questions, but she certainly couldn't understand why nearly
all the female staff and all his patients were desperately
in love with him. *She* wasn't about to fall under his spell,
that much was certain. Now, Mr Cunningham, the
senior registrar, *he* was in a different category, and Carrie
liked him. He was nearing retirement and would never
attain the giddy heights of a consultancy, but he was
popular with patients and staff alike. He was a typical
gynae—kind and understanding of women's problems
and genuinely interested in the whole person, not just in
a collection of fascinating symptoms.

Whether Mr Sheraton was genuinely interested in the
complete patient was another matter. Signs and symptoms seemed to be all that he really cared for. That, and
operations. It probably gave him a tremendous feeling of
power as he stood poised by the side of the operating
table, with knife at the ready. He was turning out to be
a tyrant and Carrie hoped he——

What she hoped she could not afterwards remember,
for when she began her perambulation along the opposite

side of the ward there was the tyrant himself, just about to sit on the bed of their oldest patient!

Mrs Sulu was a lady who had recently had a hysterectomy, and her face was wreathed in smiles now, her few remaining teeth gleaming. She was actually holding hands with Mr Sheraton, and Carrie's eyes widened. He must be unwell! No patient had ever been accorded such a privilege before.

Since he was unchaperoned, Carrie made her way briskly towards him, hoping that her reluctance didn't show.

He turned and watched her approach, and Carrie blushed before she was within speaking distance of him. She felt suddenly insignificant. Her mop of reddish-brown hair was untidy and she knew that her cap was askew. Then she remembered that she hadn't had time to polish her shoes that day. And heavens, there was a speck of patient's lunch on her starched apron! She'd meant to change it, of course, but seeing that the ward was ready for the great man had come first. Now it was too late, and she was at Mrs Sulu's bedside.

Pinning a prim smile to her face, Carrie greeted both patient and consultant, then stood with her hands clasped in front of her apron, hoping that his eagle eyes would not notice the small stain.

The eyes she had at first thought were black weren't black at all, they were a dark slate-grey, and they seemed to bore right through her and her pathetic attempt to look brisk and efficient. Not that Mr Sheraton was ever nasty, she conceded, but——

'Please tell Sister that I'm ready for my round.' With a faint smile for the beaming Mrs Sulu, the consultant got up and headed for the office, Carrie scurrying after him. But he was already in the office, gazing thoughtfully at a saucer-eyed Ann Haynes.

'I'm very sorry, sir,' Carrie said firmly, after she got her breath back, 'but Sister is at a meeting. We knew you would be delayed and——'

'And I have arrived,' Mr Sheraton finished the sentence. 'Where is Staff Nurse? Surely *you* aren't in charge of my ward?'

He raised a perfectly shaped brow in surprise, and Carrie wished crossly that everything about his features wasn't quite so perfectly shaped.

'Only for a short while, sir. Sister will be back shortly and Staff Nurse is at the dentist's. I'll bleep Sister now,' Carrie finished, wishing fervently that her senior would walk through the door.

Long, slender surgeon's fingers closed around Carrie's wrist as she reached for the phone, and she tensed, delightfully frightening sensations running up and down her spine.

'Never mind now. I suppose I will have to make do with you. I haven't time to waste.' He sighed, and Carrie almost sighed along with him.

'Yes, of course, sir,' she murmured, her mind going blank with sheer fright. Ann, though overawed, still had her wits about her, and smilingly asked the consultant to take a seat.

Carrie cursed herself for her lack of good manners, but tried to make amends by placing the Kardex in front of him.

'My registrar will see to that, thank you, Nurse. When he arrives,' Mr Sheraton said testily, pushing back the sleeve of his jacket to consult his watch. 'Where *is* everyone?'

As if at a signal, there was a tap at the door and Mr Cunningham walked in, smiling as usual. Carrie sent up a silent prayer of thanks as she saw the medical students and the houseman outside the office. Now that they were all assembled, surely the consultant could find no further fault?

Mr Sheraton found three sets of case-notes that hadn't been fully completed, and another where the latest Path Lab report was missing. Carrie wasn't responsible for the slip-up and rather thought their house officer was to blame. Of course the consultant chose to blame the nursing staff, though he didn't actually say so. The vexed expression on his face spoke volumes when he glanced at Carrie and held aloft the offending case-notes.

She met his glacial stare without flinching, but couldn't help the way her eyes sparked angrily, and a faint smile crossed the surgeon's lean face. He had a remarkably sensuous lower lip, Carrie noticed in passing, annoyed with herself for her temporary lapse. After Dr Phil Mackie, she was finished with men forever, and fully intended to devote her life to nursing. Men just did not figure in *her* future.

The round went smoothly until they reached Miss Graham, a teenager who was in for a D and C. Mr Sheraton put out a hand for the case-notes and Carrie duly placed the folder in his hand. They had two patients called Graham, but she had been extra careful and double checked that she had given him the right one.

Although the folder was the correct one, there was a note in it which belonged to the other Graham, a much older woman, and as they walked away from the bed Mr Sheraton spoke softly in Carrie's ear. Holding out a note in Sister Carter's neat handwriting, he asked smoothly, 'Why is this in Sharon Graham's folder, Nurse? It refers to her fourth pregnancy and Miss Graham hasn't had her *first* pregnancy yet.' Carrie coloured. 'Nor,' he went on relentlessly, 'is she approaching her fortieth birthday. If asked,' he continued, while Carrie yearned to slap his handsome face, 'I would say Sharon Graham wasn't even twenty yet. About your own age, I would think?'

Carrie resolutely ignored the question in his voice as she murmured an apology for the mis-filing. Since they had a ward clerk, the error was hardly hers, but consultants didn't care; just as long as they could wipe the floor with someone, they were perfectly happy. It was another black mark for Marigold Ward and another one for Student Nurse Carrie West, who couldn't afford any

more. The high jinks following her last party would not
be forgotten—or forgiven—for a very long time.

Mr Sheraton sat staring pensively into space once they
were back in the office. Although it was a large room,
there weren't chairs enough for everyone, and the small
group of medical students stood against the wall, like
prisoners awaiting the firing-squad, Carrie thought fan-
cifully. They didn't dare lounge against the wall, as she
had seen them do on other consultants' rounds, and they
all—except one—stared anxiously at Mr Sheraton, each
one wondering if he or she were to be questioned, no
doubt.

The exception was a big, gangling boy named Terry
Hammond, who had developed a penchant for Carrie,
the more so since she was no longer seen in the company
of Phil Mackie. She did nothing to encourage him, but,
being kind hearted, did not actively discourage him as
some nurses might have done.

Terry winked at her behind the surgeon's back and
Carrie shook her head warningly. That was the kind of
problem she could do without! Unfortunately, Robert
Sheraton chose that moment to glance up, and his
pensive expression rapidly turned thunderous.

Terry visibly wilted, and Carrie felt sorry for him. Mr
Sheraton took his revenge by asking him several questions about the patients—questions to which the student
clearly didn't know the answers. Despite the awe in
which they all held the consultant, Terry was a lazy boy
and must have spent the round thinking about Carrie.

It cost him dear, though, and Carrie felt each blow
which was aimed at him. If Mr Sheraton had taken a
stick and beaten him, Terry could not have suffered
more, and Carrie wondered miserably when her own
turn would come. It wasn't likely that he would reprimand her personally. Consultants didn't work like that.
They were hidebound creatures who went through the
proper channels—everyone knew that. First, he would
speak to Sister, who would tell the surgical nursing

officer. And so it would go on all through the ranks until it reached the chief herself. Carrie could well picture *that* scene.

Mr Sheraton had returned to routine matters, and Carrie dragged her mind back from visions of the bleak future which awaited her. Uncle Charles would go berserk, that was for certain. Already he and Aunt Moira were——

But she had overestimated Mr Sheraton's hidebound propensities. 'Tell my students about myomectomies, Nurse,' he invited, and there was a deafening silence as everyone turned to look at her.

'It's—it's the removal of fibroids, sir!' Carrie blurted out, wishing the floor would open up and swallow her.

'Tell us a little more, Nurse.' Mr Sheraton was actually smiling, Carrie saw with surprise. He had a rather nice smile, though of course it was all a sham. The man was trying to trip her up.

Well, she wouldn't let him! 'It's the shelling out of fibroids through an incision in the wall of the uterus, sir,' she said firmly.

'A myomectomy is the shelling out of fibroids,' Mr Sheraton agreed softly. 'And what might be the complications of such an operation?' he went on, his cool gaze quelling Terry Hammond, who was smiling encouragingly at Carrie.

'Haemorrhage, sir,' Carrie went on quickly. She wasn't sure about that, but it was always safe to assume that bleeding post-operatively might be a problem. 'Oh, and severe pain. Mrs Jordan suffered quite a lot of pain at first,' she continued, feeling on safer ground now as she related the disorder and the symptoms to a specific patient. 'And she had difficulty in passing urine, too.'

'Good,' Mr Sheraton approved. 'Someone knows her job, I'm glad to see. Now. . .' He paused, while Carrie struggled to face the fact that he was actually praising her! 'Miss Graham and Mrs Jordan for discharge, I think. Do you agree?'

Carrie stared. The surgeon was looking at her expectantly. Never having been asked if she agreed with a consultant's views before, she was temporarily at a loss. Then she remembered Mrs Jordan's home circumstances.

'No! They've just lost their flat, sir. The Jordans, I mean. He was behind with the rent. The arrears were dreadful but he said it wasn't his fault because——'

'Does your tortuous answer imply that my patient has nowhere to go?'

'Yes, sir,' muttered Carrie. 'She hasn't anywhere to go.' Mr Jordan was staying temporarily with his married sister in a high-rise flat. There wasn't room for his wife, though.

'We haven't room to keep her here, sir,' the jovial Mr Cunningham put in, and the consultant nodded absently. He drummed his fingers against Sister's desk for a moment, deep in thought. Otherwise the office was silent, waiting for the great man to speak.

At last he glanced up, his eyes shadowed. 'Is there room on Primula Ward?'

Primula was the other, smaller gynae ward, and it also had a waiting-list as long as Carrie's arm. She shook her head, the bright curls dancing. 'I'm afraid Primula is full, sir. Perhaps we could find a vacancy in general surgery?' she ventured, as keen as the surgeons to find somewhere for the sweet Mrs Jordan.

It was finally decided that the hospital social workers be pressed to do something about the Jordans' problems, and the round broke up soon afterwards, still with no sign of Sister Carter. She would be furious at missing Mr Sheraton, and there was no doubt in Carrie's mind whose head would roll as a result.

Sister Carter fancied the cold, cynical Mr Sheraton, and he had, in fact, taken her out to dinner the previous week. Carrie had that information hot from the grapevine. Probably, being a cold fish, the man had wanted to discuss bed states and operations, but Sister had come on duty actually *smiling* the following morning, so there might be more to Robert Sheraton than met the eye. Though where that left his wife, she of the laser eyes, Carrie had no idea. Consultants had to be careful about allowing no hint of scandal to blemish their private lives, and it seemed strange that a married consultant would wine and dine a ward sister, but no doubt Sister had read more into the outing than Mr Sheraton had intended.

Carrie shot him a quick glance from under her gold-tipped lashes as he dismissed the students. He didn't *look* passionate and—— Meeting the consultant's gaze was like being unexpectedly ducked in an Arctic stream, and Carrie decided that no passion lurked behind *that* glacial exterior. And, glancing around in surprise, she saw that even Mr Cunningham had departed, leaving her alone with the boss.

Feeling suddenly nervous, she fiddled with the case-notes in front of her. She sat in Sister Carter's seat, while the consultant lounged in the comfortable armchair opposite. If she put out her hand, she could touch him, and the thought was frightening in a delicious sort of way.

Carrie forced herself to speak. 'Are there any messages for Sister, sir? Or should I bleep her now? She will be sorry——'

'She isn't the only one who will be sorry.' The words were softly spoken but were full of hidden menace. At least it seemed that way to Carrie. 'If you cannot keep *your* mind on the patients, perhaps you should spare a thought for the medical students,' Mr Sheraton continued in that same gentle, conversational tone. 'Young Hammond is a doctor of the future. If he allows himself to be distracted by pretty young girls with big green eyes, he'll never make the grade.'

Carrie nodded in agreement, surprised and pleased that he should consider her pretty. 'Yes, sir,' she added for good measure.

'Therefore, Nurse——' He leaned nearer to read her name-badge, and Carrie tried to prevent herself from leaning back against the wall. 'Nurse West,' he continued, 'you are preventing a doctor of the future from carrying out his duties. Perhaps even preventing him from *ever* becoming a doctor, since women were put on this earth solely to distract men,' he added drily.

That was too much. 'But I didn't!'

Mr Sheraton continued as if she hadn't interrupted. 'If I catch you distracting any of my team in the future, I shall——'

'No, you won't!' Carrie exploded. She shot out of the chair and glared down at the bemused surgeon. 'I was not distracting Terry Hammond! He winked at me and I shook my head,' she went on in a quieter tone.

'Ah, I see! A case of "not tonight, Josephine". No doubt you will plan an assignation for a more convenient night?' Robert Sheraton suggested.

The implication of his words wasn't lost on Carrie, who flared up again. 'I think you're insufferable!' she said hotly. Then she realised that she was speaking to a consultant, and went crimson, then white, then crimson again. She could actually *feel* the colour changes. Her eyes mirrored her horror as she gazed down at the consultant, who had remained seated, a faint smile lurking about his mobile mouth.

'I—I'm very sorry, sir,' Carrie muttered, wondering if she would be given a month's notice or thrown out immediately. *Could* they throw a learner out like that? she wondered in passing.

Slate-grey eyes met hers. Mr Sheraton's expression was unfathomable, and if he was angry he was concealing it extremely well. 'Tell Sister that Mrs Jordan is for discharge when suitable arrangements have been made. Thank you.' He rose, and, with a distant nod, walked out.

Carrie collapsed into Sister's chair, and was still there,

head buried in her hands, when Sister Carter walked in a few moments later.

'Nurse West!'

Carrie flinched at the voice of authority, and hurriedly vacated Sister's chair. 'Sorry, Sister! I—Mr Sheraton was here just now!' she blurted out, and the tall, blonde Sister clicked her tongue reproachfully.

'I know, I met him in the corridor. *Why* did I have to meet Mr Sheraton in the corridor, Nurse?' Sister demanded, settling herself elegantly behind her desk. 'Directly he came, you should have bleeped me,' she went on sharply. 'Consultants can't be expected to conduct a round with a second-year student in charge! You're only *just* second year, after all, and if it hadn't been for that wretched virus going around I wouldn't have had to leave you in charge.'

Carrie winced. 'I tried to bleep you, but he wouldn't let me,' she said, aggrieved. 'He said not to bother——' And he put out his hand and gripped my wrist and I enjoyed the contact—that was what *really* happened, Sister! Carrie bit her lip, wondering what Sister would say if she dared speak that aloud!

It was true, she had enjoyed the contact. Mr Sheraton was so unlike Phil Mackie, and Terry, and all the other boys who seemed to fancy her. That was the trouble—they were boys and he was very definitely a man! Her face clouded. Likeable though they were, once they reached registrar's rank they changed, and not for the better.

'If you could bring your scattered wits back to me, I would be obliged, Nurse West.' Sister's pale eyes rested on Carrie suspiciously, and with an effort she began to brief her senior on the round.

When the briefing was over, Sister leaned back in her chair, a smile lurking in her eyes. 'Now, Nurse, perhaps you would tell me what put Mr Sheraton in such a foul mood?'

Carrie's eyes widened. 'I thought he was always in a foul mood, Sister,' she said, and Sister's lips tightened.

'This was far worse than I've seen. He was positively foaming at the mouth,' Siser went on reflectively. '*Do* tell me, Nurse. If you've upset him, you will have to apologise.'

Sister Carter did not appear angry. In fact, she looked rather pleased as Carrie hesitantly poured out the sad tale, not forgetting to mention the medical student, though she didn't name him. She wondered if sister and surgeon had quarrelled. Perhaps Sister Carter had been superseded in the man's regard. The grapevine hadn't throbbed with any more news about him, but even so. . .

'I suppose you encouraged the student. You young nurses always do,' Sister sighed, and Carrie didn't try to correct her. 'Now, you had better find Mr Sheraton and apologise. Can't have him thinking we condone that sort of behaviour on Marigold, can we? Go straight away, Nurse. Strike while the iron's hot.'

Certainly Carrie could see the sense in apologising to the consultant—before he had a chance to complain to the tutorial staff. It was strange he hadn't complained to Sister Carter, Carrie mused as she set off in pursuit of him. Perhaps he was the type of man who enjoyed brooding for a day or so, then—wham! Keeping the victim in suspense was a particularly nasty trait, she considered, and it saddened her to think that Mr Sheraton was like that.

St Hilda's was an old and distinguished hospital, situated just outside the town of Gainsborough in the Sussex Weald, and many of the buildings dated back to the turn of the century. Others had been added later, like the admin offices, where, Carrie hoped, the surgeon might be found. The admin block was separate from the main building, and to get there she had to walk along what seemed a mile of chilly corridor, then go out through a side-door and dash across to the long, low building.

If the main hospital was cold enough, Admin was worse, little more than sub-zero, Carrie felt, as she gathered her navy cape more closely about her, mid-February not being the best time for venturing away from the wards.

She hurried past numbered but otherwise anonymous offices until she reached the other end of the building, then emerged a few moments later from the secretary's office, with the prospect of more detective work ahead of her. Mr Sheraton should be taking his obstetric out-patient clinic, but his secretary thought Mr Cunningham might be taking it instead.

'Mr Sheraton wasn't himself when he came in to dictate his letters,' his middle-aged secretary said, and Carrie flushed. If he wasn't himself, there could be only one cause—Nurse Caroline West!

Feeling more of a criminal by the minute, Carrie hurried to the slightly warmer out-patient clinics. The consultant *was* taking his clinic, it seemed, and Carrie settled down on a bench to await the man. She shivered and snuggled into her cape, rather wishing it were a magic carpet which would carry her far, far away from a certain consultant gynaecologist!

CHAPTER THREE

THE patient was in with the consultant a long time, and Carrie grew more apprehensive by the minute. It was like taking examinations all over again, only ten times worse!

So tense was she that she almost shot out of her seat when the beaming mother-to-be emerged. 'He's lovely, isn't he?' the woman enthused, and Carrie nodded dully. 'So kind and understanding,' the woman went on. '*He* didn't tell me I was a fool to start a family at forty-one!'

It cheered Carrie up immensely to know that Mr Sheraton wasn't quite the ogre she had thought. He did understand the older woman's feelings. She only hoped he would be as considerate of the feelings of a much younger one.

Bracing herself, Carrie knocked at the door of the examination room. At the abrupt command to enter, she did so, gingerly pushing the door open. Then, ashamed of her timidity, she tilted her head proudly and sailed right up to the desk where the consultant was writing.

The staff nurse turned to stare at her, and Carrie smiled winningly. 'I have a personal message for Mr Sheraton please, Staff.' The nurse nodded and, to Carrie's relief, went out, closing the door behind her.

Robert Sheraton glanced up, eyes narrowing when they rested upon Carrie. 'Yes, Nurse? What message is there?'

'I—it was an apology, sir,' Carrie said in surprise. There was no recognition in the surgeon's eyes. Surely he couldn't have forgotten the saucy Nurse West already? And here she was reminding him!

'An apology?' He sounded weary as he ran his fingers through his black hair, leaving it even untidier. Carrie's eyes strayed to the enormous pile of papers on his desk. The white coat he wore was open, so was the top button of his shirt, and the elegant grey tie he'd worn at the ward round was discarded. 'Well? Go on, Nurse. I haven't all day to waste.' Mr Sheraton's tone was testy, and Carrie nibbled her lower lip anxiously as those dark eyes homed in on her.

'Please, Mr Sheraton. Sister sent me to apologise for— for the trouble I caused. For being rude to you. I'm from Marigold Ward, sir.' Carrie added, since he still did not appear to recognise her.

'Ah, yes! Marigold Ward. Did you cause me trouble, Nurse?' There was the faintest of smiles on his face, and Carrie flushed. He remembered her very well!

'Sister Carter said you were in—were cross,' Carrie blundered on, having nearly told him he was in a foul mood, 'and she said I must apologise and hope you wouldn't take the matter further.' There, that was the message she had been sent to deliver, so now she ought to go while the going was good. And yet. . .

'I'm sure it's of no consequence now.' Mr Sheraton bestowed a faint smile upon her before picking up his pen again, thus signalling that the interview was over.

'And I want to thank you for coming to our rescue just before Christmas,' Carrie went on, ignoring the faint sigh that emanated from him. 'You won't remember me, but you were our Good Samaritan and I didn't have time to thank you, so I have now,' she finished swiftly, beaming at the consultant, then making for the door before he could snarl at her.

'I *do* recall a young lady with foxy-coloured hair and big green eyes, as it happens.' Mr Sheraton's mild voice stopped Carrie in her tracks. Far from snarling, the man was actually smiling!

'Oh! Well, I'm glad. I *did* thank your wife but I didn't get around to——'

'Ah, yes, my wife. Yes, you did thank her, didn't you?' Mr Sheraton sounded wary, and Carrie's eyes narrowed.

'She was someone else's wife?' she guessed, and Mr

Sheraton made a sound which was somewhere between a laugh and a snarl.

'Get out while you're still in one piece, Nurse West,' he advised, but laughter lurked in his eyes, and Carrie chuckled, before making her escape. The man was human, after all!

Sister Carter seemed vexed at the consultant's response to the apology, but she didn't insist that the tutors be informed, and Carrie heaved a sigh of relief. She had escaped this time, but vowed to keep out of Mr Sheraton's way for the next few weeks, just to be on the safe side!

She had the weekend off, something of a rare event, and she spent Saturday morning with Ann and several others. They all held a study bee in Carrie's room in the nurses' home, six of them squashed into a space hardly adequate for one. Since they were all based on surgical wards, the discussion was mainly about ops, but it soon petered out, and Carrie found to her dismay that they wanted to hear about the dishy Robert Sheraton.

Since she was happy to talk about him, she really should not have minded, yet she did. He was *her* consultant and she couldn't see why the others should take such an interest. They couldn't *all* be in love with him!

One student was, at least, or thought she was, and she proudly informed them that Mr Sheraton had actually smiled at her! There was a chorus of dissent.

'The man never smiles at *anyone*!'

'You're making it up to upset us!'

'He was snarling, I expect. You were probably standing on his corns,' another girl put in, waving a hand vaguely to indicate the girl's heavyweight form.

Carrie thought that remark unkind and didn't hesitate to say so. 'He might have been smiling,' she went on, doubt in her voice. 'I've never actually seen him smile,' she lied, 'though he sits on patients' beds and gazes soulfully into their eyes,' she added, with a grin.

It was Ann Haynes who supplied a piece of information about him for Carrie to add to her meagre store. 'He wouldn't be interested in anyone in this room,' she said importantly. '*I* know who he's dating now!'

The chorus urged her to tell, only Carrie remaining silent. She didn't *care* whom Mr Sheraton was dating. Nevertheless, she expressed as much surprise as the rest when she found out. 'Sister Whitworth! *Is* he?

'Our Peg is lovely, but——'

'She was awfully kind to me when I did obstetrics.'

'She's hardly *his* type, though.'

Carrie fully agreed with all that was said. Sister Peggy Whitworth was a sister midwife. Short, plump and sweet-natured, she was a great favourite with mothers, babies and staff. Yet somehow Carrie couldn't see the austere Robert Sheraton taking her out. 'I can't really see them hitting it off,' she said morosely.

'I *saw* them! I told you, they were going into the Barbican. Sister Whitworth saw me and waved, so I know it was her, and there's no possibility of mistaking him,' Ann went on smugly.

Mr Sheraton and Sister Whitworth. 'An unlikely combination,' Carrie said firmly.

'Not so unlikely,' one of the others said. 'She's a midwife and he's an obstetrician. They were made for each other. *I* think it's romantic,' she sighed, and the others giggled, before Ann said thoughtfully.

'He isn't married already, I suppose? Consultants usually are, and I can't see a guy as handsome as that being single. Phil says——'

'I don't suppose Phil knows any more than the rest of us,' Carrie interposed swiftly. 'Yes, he probably *is* married.'

'Unless he's gay!'

Five pairs of eyes glared at their colleague, who subsided. Then, reluctantly putting aside thoughts of the dishy Mr Sheraton, the girls settled down to their studying.

Peggy Whitworth was more suitable for Mr Sheraton than the sometimes mean-minded Sister Carter, Carrie acknowledged later, as she and Ann sat wrestling with gynae problems, the other students having dispersed.

'Oh, Carrie, before I forget—will you take Phil shopping for me on Monday?' Ann's light, pleasant voice broke in on Carrie's muddled thoughts, and she stared at her friend.

'Take Phil shopping? Me?' Didn't Ann know what she was asking?

Ann probably didn't realise just how fond Carrie had been of Dr Phil Mackie. Indeed, once she had fancied herself in love with the houseman from cardiology, and once Phil had whispered sweet words of affection, if not love, into her ear. Then suddenly it was over, and Phil had started dating Ann, to Carrie's astonishment.

She was too proud to ask him why he had changed girlfriends so abruptly. She was never short of admirers, but nevertheless his cold-blooded defection had hurt. She really believed she had loved him. What made matters worse was that in no time at all Phil and Ann got engaged! The wedding was planned for the end of next year, after Ann had taken her finals.

Perhaps it had been love at first sight for them both, but being left so suddenly and without explanation still hurt Carrie, and she certainly had no intention of going shopping with him. Presumably it was to chose a twenty-first birthday present for Ann.

It was, and Ann wouldn't accept Carrie's cool refusal. 'Why can't you?' she cried. Her eyes were rapidly filling with tears, and Carrie felt awful. If she explained that she had once loved Phil, maybe still did, Ann would be hurt. Phil was the only romance in Ann's life, and Carrie didn't want to spoil it for her.

'I can't take someone else's fiancé shopping! People will talk,' she said crossly, but Ann was blithely unconcerned.

'You mean because you and Phil used to go around

together? But there was nothing in that! Phil told me himself you had some good times but he never really fancied you! Oh!' Ann stopped in consternation.

'It's all right, Ann. We were just buddies,' Carrie hastened to assure her friend, at the same time thinking dark thoughts of a certain houseman.

'Well, yes, that's what Phil said. I didn't mean that he didn't fancy you. What I meant was he never——'

'Never mind.' Carrie stood up and stretched her cramped legs. The desk and chair which were crammed into a corner of the room were more suitable for an infants' classroom, she felt. How the much taller Ann managed to squeeze behind her own desk Carrie couldn't imagine. 'Phil and I had a friendship. That's all,' she added. 'I'll take him shopping—if he doesn't mind?'

'Well—I haven't actually asked him,' Ann admitted. 'But I know he'll need help. You know what men are!'

Carrie silently agreed that yes, indeed, she *did* know what men were. Hadn't she suffered a broken heart twice? Wondering what was wrong with her that men could cast her aside so easily, and whether Mr Sheraton had noticed it, she agreed to meet Phil on Monday morning, since she wouldn't be on duty until twelve-thirty that day.

But first there was the ordeal of the Sunday lunch to be faced, and Carrie's heart sank like a stone. Her father had remarried when she was twelve and now lived in London. They kept in touch and she still saw him occasionally, but it was her mother's brother who had taken over the responsibility for the young Carrie, and her sister, Judy, who was six years older.

Uncle Charles and Aunt Moira had done their best to make Carrie feel at home, and she knew she should be grateful, but, thanks largely to her aunt, she had never felt really comfortable there. It was with a sense of relief that she had chosen to live in the nurses' home the moment she commenced training. But since Uncle Charles was otherwise known as Dr Charles Warriner, the consultant pathologist at St Hilda's, he and his wife still took a keen interest in her affairs and seemed not to realise that she was well able to take care of herself. Her aunt lectured her every time she obeyed the summons to spend Sunday with them, and she was usually only too glad to work weekends just to escape the ordeal.

It was bitterly cold when she set out to walk to the Warriners' house, and she was muffled up in a quilted coat Judy had sent her for Christmas. It was two sizes too big but that left plenty of room for jumpers, and Carrie wore three plus her thermal underwear, a pair of thick tights, heavyweight socks *and* her sturdy wellingtons. A jaunty tasselled cap was pulled well down over her ears, and she just hoped she wouldn't meet anyone she knew!

There had been a light fall of snow in the night, just enough to cover the pavements and leave a light scattering on the Downs, and a thin film of ice had formed, making walking treacherous. Carrie chose to walk in the road, turning her head every now and again in case a car came up without her hearing it.

The square where her uncle lived was quiet and well off the main road, and Carrie didn't expect there to be a sudden surge of motorists. She was taken by surprise when she heard the soft purring of an engine not far behind, and quickly headed for the pavement, lost her footing and fell into the gutter.

Shaking her head to clear it, she remained on all fours for a moment, mentally assessing whether or not she had broken anything, the motorist already forgotten. She had just decided that she hadn't broken her leg *or* her wrist, when she heard a car door slam, and a pair of strong hands gripped her shoulders.

'Are you hurt? Don't move until I see whether you've broken anything. I'm a doctor,' the voice added—a dark brown voice Carrie knew only too well.

'No, I'm perfectly all right, thank you. Just shaken, that's all.' Carrie shook off his hands and attempted to rise, keeping her face averted, and glad that her cap covered her reddish hair. Mr Sheraton would certainly remember her hair! 'Really, I'm fine,' she mumbled. 'Thank you for stopping. Goodbye!'

She walked slowly and carefully away, anxious not to have another fall, and had reached the sanctuary of her uncle's gateway before she realised that she wasn't alone—her rescuer was right behind her.

'I'm perfectly all right!' Her voice was sharp, and she panicked, determined not to turn around. 'There's no need, really!'

'I'd be failing in my duty as a Good Samaritan if I didn't see you safely indoors,' Mr Sheraton's amused voice said, and Carrie could have cried.

'Oh!' she said, whirling round to face him. The man was actually laughing at her! She knew she was staring but couldn't help it. The surgeon looked years younger when he laughed, those slate-grey eyes positively glowing, and Carrie could feel the swift tide of colour that crept up from her neck and made its agonisingly slow way up to her brow. 'I'm—I'm all right now, thank you, sir,' she muttered, wishing it were anyone but he who had seen her dressed in mountains of old clothes.

'In that case, I'll go back to my car and park it properly. I'm lunching with the Warriners,' he went on slowly. 'Are you some relation?'

Carrie swallowed. 'Yes, I'm Dr Warriner's niece. *I'm* having lunch with them, too.' She tried to look beyond Mr Sheraton but couldn't see his car—was he bringing a female friend to lunch, by some chance? And, if so, which one?

Since she could hardly ask him, Carrie contented herself with giving him a vague smile, before ringing the doorbell. As the door opened, she cast a furtive glance over her shoulder and was relieved to find that he had disappeared from view.

'Caroline, dear! What have you been up to?' Aunt Moira surveyed Carrie without enthusiasm.

'I slipped and fell, Aunt Moira, but I'm all right. I met Mr Sheraton—he's just coming in. He had to park his car because——' Carrie stopped, cursing her wayward tongue. No, she certainly wasn't going to tell her aunt that Mr Sheraton had to re-park his car because of her!

'Oh, is Robert on his way? Was he alone?'

Carrie edged herself in through the door, since her aunt seemed disposed to hang about waiting for the consultant. 'I don't know, I think so. Oh, hello, Uncle Charles!'

Carrie greeted her uncle with rather more warmth than she had his wife. Because she was aware of the fact, she felt guilty, but it was difficult trying to feel affection for a woman who constantly found fault with her.

'Hello, puss. Been keeping the patients happy, then? From what I hear, you're a regular live wire!' Her uncle chuckled then patted her affectionately on the cheek.

Carrie smiled up at him. It had to be said that she preferred her uncle to her own father, who had always seemed to her to be wrapped up in his own life and had little time to spare for the problems of his children, not even Judy, who was undoubtedly his favourite.

Shrugging aside the thought, Carrie almost tore off her coat and the numerous jumpers, not wanting the surgeon to see her at her worst. But then, he always saw her at her worst, that was the trouble. It wasn't that his opinion mattered all that much—not personally, that was. But a consultant's opinion carried a lot of weight when it came to professional matters, and Carrie was already in the bad books of the tutors, of Sister Carter, *and* of the home warden, and if she fell foul of Mr Sheraton as well her days at St Hilda's were numbered.

Cast into gloom by the thought, she fussed over the Warriners' pet Yorkie, an elderly and rather deaf bitch who rejoiced in the name of 'Girlie'. Girlie, who was twelve and overweight but still thought she was a puppy, gave Carrie's hands a good lick then began to lick her tights for good measure, then hastily abandoned her when she heard someone else being greeted by her mistress.

Carrie watched in amazement as the debonair Robert Sheraton was accorded the same treatment as herself. Indeed, the dog gazed up at the surgeon, wagging her stump of a tail and yapping excitedly, before trying to lick his hand. Carrie considered that Girlie showed a distinct lack of judgement, and was behaving like an over-excited fan at a pop concert. If Mr Sheraton repulsed her, she would have only herself to blame.

But he didn't. Instead, he lifted the old dog on to his lap and began to pull her ear, whereupon Girlie rolled over on to her back and gazed up at him so lovingly that Carrie couldn't help laughing.

The surgeon's dark gaze was transferred to her, and Carrie rather wished she could feel his long, sensitive fingers pulling *her* ear. Then she blushed, hoping he didn't read minds, particularly the mind of one foolish student nurse!

'You're on your own, then, Robert? Mireille couldn't come?' Aunt Moira sounded pleased, for some reason, and Carrie wondered who Mireille was. Certainly she couldn't be the woman who was with him last Christmas, because he had almost admitted that she was someone else's wife and he would hardly bring her to meet Aunt Moira.

Mr Sheraton shook his head, his gaze still fixed thoughtfully on Carrie. 'I decided against bringing her. She hasn't really shaken off the flu and she wasn't keen to come out, I'm afraid. She sends her apologies,' he added, probably as an afterthought, Carrie reflected. This Mireille probably knew she was in for a boring lunch, with the two men talking shop as they inevitably would.

'We've a surprise for you, Caroline,' her aunt broke into Carrie's thoughts.

'Oh? Something nice?' For politeness' sake, Carrie forced enthusiasm into her voice.

'Yes, I'm sure it will be pleasant, but—but it hasn't happened yet.' Aunt Moira's voice trailed off as her husband gave her a look.

'Is it going to happen while I'm here?' Robert Sheraton sounded faintly amused.

'Well, I had hoped so, but time's getting on,' Aunt Moira said vaguely, waving a hand towards the door, and Carrie was immediately alert.

'It isn't Dad, is it? Is he coming to lunch?' She kept her voice level, expressionless, or so she hoped.

'Typical,' Uncle Charles said quietly. 'No, it isn't your father, Carrie, it's Judy. Moira thought she might make it in time for lunch. She's coming to spend a few days with us. At least, she hasn't *said* so, but. . .' He shrugged.

'She never does,' Carrie put in. 'It's a case of expect her when you see her, isn't it? I wish you'd told me— I've still got one of her jumpers and I could have brought it with me.' Her sister lived in London now, near their father, and Carrie rarely saw her. When they met, it was usually in London, since Judy hated what she called the 'parish-pump mentality' of Gainsborough and the sur- rounding country.

'I dare say she's got enough jumpers without the one she loaned you,' Uncle Charles said drily, and Carrie laughed. Seeing the quizzing expression on Mr Sheraton's face, she added, 'Judy's my sister and she's got loads of clothes! She buys something new every week, I think. And every time she makes a sale she sends me the money for a new outfit. She writes books,' Carrie added, in case the surgeon might not know. 'She isn't famous yet but she will be, I'm sure of it!'

'I'm sure you're right,' Mr Sheraton said gently, then he turned to his hostess, leaving Carrie with the suspicion that he wasn't the slightest bit interested in her clever sister. Well, he would be if he saw her! That thought rather dampened Carrie's enthusiasm. Yes, if Mr Sheraton saw Judy he wouldn't care *what* she did for a living, he would simply stare in open admiration. Men always did that, and both sisters thought it a great joke, for, although stunningly beautiful, Judy was completely without vanity.

Carrie's eyes shadowed. Yes, she was fond of Judy, but she would rather her sister arrived *after* Mr Robert Sheraton had left!

CHAPTER FOUR

FORTUNATELY for Carrie's peace of mind, her sister didn't turn up during Sunday lunch, and she spent a more enjoyable afternoon than she had expected. This was largely due to the efforts made by Robert Sheraton, who was a perfect guest. He had apparently pushed to the back of his mind the fact that his fellow guest was that troublesome Student Nurse West, and he actually treated her as an equal. Someone of equal intellectual ability as well as a social equal, Carrie found to her surprise.

It was something new for her, and she revelled in it, blossoming out in a way she never could in Judy's presence or their father's. With them, she felt she was insignificant, a mere nurse rather than someone who was on the fringes of show business, since their father was a noted lecturer and had frequently appeared on television, and Judy looked set to follow him. A nurse counted for less than nothing in that world, though Carrie knew it wasn't really so. A TV personality wouldn't be much use to anyone who needed nursing or had broken a leg!

No, she wasn't really insignificant and her job really *was* worthwhile, but she never really felt at home with non-nursing or medical people. With Mr Sheraton it was different, and Carrie forgot how big was the divide between consultant and student nurse. It took her aunt Moira to point *that* out.

'Caroline, dear, don't interrupt Mr Sheraton. He wants to explain something to your uncle.' This was during the coffee afterwards, when they all lazed around in the cosy drawing room of the Warriners' big house. Mr Sheraton himself was sprawled comfortably at one

40

end of the settee, with Carrie sitting primly at the other end and Girlie lying between them.

'Sorry,' Carrie murmured, 'but I——'

'That's quite enough, Caroline!' Aunt Moira's voice was sharp, as she rose. 'Come and help me rinse the cups, there's a good girl. The men want to talk shop.'

'Don't whisk Nurse West away on my account,' Mr Sheraton said lightly. 'She's interested in talking shop as well—aren't you, Nurse?'

Carrie nodded, then hastily picked up the cups and saucers, carrying them over to her aunt, who was waiting to wheel the trolley out to the kitchen.

'Really, Caroline! You were rather familiar with Mr Sheraton, you know. Consultants don't like pert nurses.' The cups were treated harshly as Aunt Moira took out her ill humour on them, and Carrie frowned behind her back.

'Sorry, I didn't think,' she said lightly, determined not to let her aunt upset what had been a perfect day. She knew Aunt Moira wasn't all that well, and frequently complained of tiredness, and would have offered to wash up for her if she hadn't known in advance that such an offer would have been declined out of hand.

'That's just it—you never think! You seem to be in trouble with everyone at the hospital! You can imagine how embarrassing it is for your uncle. Anyone would think you hadn't an ounce of common sense, and I shudder to think how your poor patients manage. No——' Aunt Moira held up a hand as Carrie went swiftly to defend herself '—spare me the details; you know I've never been a nurse. I *have* been a patient, though, and let me tell you——'

Carrie was spared being told whatever it was, for the consultant, *both* consultants, appeared in the doorway, and Robert Sheraton was smiling down at her in a way that caused the last vestiges of Carrie's common sense to leave her completely. The saucer she was drying slipped out of her fingers and smashed on the floor.

Before her aunt could give both men an account of
Caroline's many faults, Mr Sheraton was in the kitchen,
bending down and helping Carrie to pick up the shards
of china. They both reached for the same piece but
Carrie managed to snatch her hand away in time, so
fortunately she and the surgeon didn't come into physical
contact, but it was as though they had. *Something* passed
between them—what, Carrie didn't know. Probably it
was only a wave of sympathy. He must have heard her
aunt's shrill voice bemoaning her lack of sense. Yes, that
was it, he felt sorry for her. Maybe he'd had a relative
like that when he was young.

Sympathy was all very well, but Carrie didn't intend
to become an object of pity, so she smiled in her usual
sunny manner, thanked the consultant prettily for helping her, then apologised to her aunt, offering to replace
the broken item.

'Well, I don't think you can.' Aunt Moira's voice was
more moderate now. 'Never mind, what's done is done
and can't be mended. That's what my mother used to
say! You run along and get your coat and Charles will
give you a lift back.

Disappointment flooded Carrie. 'Oh, is it that time
already? Oh, heavens!' One glance at her watch confirmed Carrie's worst fears. She had a case-study to write
for the tutor, and, since it had to be in by tomorrow and
she hadn't even begun it yet, the sooner she left, the
better. It served her right, hanging on just to spend more
time with Mr Sheraton. Now she would have to sit up
half the night to get it finished—well, *begun*, anyway—
then she had to go out with Phil before duty tomorrow.

The future looked so black that Carrie preferred not
to think about it. Instead, she hurried away to get her
coat and all her woollies, wondering what Mr Sheraton
would be doing once he left them. Would the mysterious
Mireille want a detailed breakdown of the afternoon?
Would she laugh when she heard about Nurse West and
the mountain of clothes she wore?

Carrie was just wallowing in a positive orgy of self-pity when the day once more took a turn for the better. She was to be driven back to the hospital, but not by Uncle Charles, by Robert Sheraton!

'I expect you're anxious to get back, puss,' her uncle said genially. 'If I know you, there's some studying you simply *must* do!' He laughed, but Carrie flushed. His remark was only too accurate!

'Not studying, exactly, but I have to write a case-study,' she admitted. Risking a glance at Mr Sheraton, she surprised that thoughtful expression on his face again, and she supposed miserably that he must be wondering whether she spent *all* her time skimping her studies and leaving everything to the last moment.

Being aware that there was some truth in that supposition didn't make Carrie feel any better, and there was an awkward silence between them as she and the consultant walked out to his car, the BMW in which Mr Sheraton, in the guise of a Good Samaritan, had helped her out that December evening.

How long ago that seemed. Then, she and Phil Mackie were friends, good friends, and there seemed every possibility that something deeper might develop. Now, just two short months later, Phil was engaged to marry someone else, her best friend, and she was alone again. Oh, well, it made studying for her exams that much easier. Phil had demanded too much of her attention, and, being a naturally gregarious girl, Carrie had enjoyed going out to parties with him, shopping in London, sightseeing, discos. Life was simpler without his teasing presence but it was certainly duller.

'You're deep in thought, Carrie.' Robert Sheraton's deep, resonant voice broke into her thoughts, and Carrie started, her eyes widening. He had called her Carrie!

They were under way now, and Carrie turned to wave to Uncle Charles but he had already gone back inside the warm house, and she couldn't blame him. Yet, glancing back at the closed door, Carrie felt a stab of what seemed to be homesickness. Yet, how could that be? It wasn't her home, not really. She supposed it must be the long winter, plus the fact that Judy was coming to stay.

'I was just thinking about Judy, my sister, sir,' she murmured, reluctant to break the silence in case they came to verbal blows. 'I miss her—we don't see each other very much,' she explained.

'I doubt that you have much in common,' the surgeon commented, as he turned right into the long, winding road that rejoiced in the name of Hospital Road. 'She sounds as if she's well on the way to making her first million!'

'If she is, she'll give me some of it,' Carrie said confidently, and was surprised and disconcerted by the surgeon's chuckle. It was a deep, throaty sort of chuckle and she rather liked it. Then she remembered Mireille and subsided again, hunching herself into her quilted coat, and thinking about the case-study.

At least, she tried to think about her case-study, but the surgeon's laughing eyes *would* intrude. And she could hear his chuckle long after he had set her down right at the door of the nurses' home.

'It's the least I can do since I unceremoniously dumped you on a doorstep last time I gave you a lift,' he said lightly, and Carrie's eyes brightened. He remembered very well, then!

'Thank you! I—is Mireille your wife?' she blurted out.

Mr Sheraton didn't answer, merely got out and opened the car door for her before Carrie could move to do it for herself. 'Out you get, Nurse West, and get on with that case-study!'

He smiled down at her, a tall, lean man in a sheepskin jacket, bare-headed and looking so much younger, more carefree than he did on the ward. Carrie swallowed the lump in her throat and tried to thank him.

He brushed her thanks aside, told her to take care, then got into his car again, Carrie watching it until the lights disappeared. Then, frozen to the marrow, she made her reluctant way into the nurses' home, its air of bleak anonymity seeming even bleaker.

Ann had arranged for Phil Mackie to meet Carrie in the High Street at ten o'clock the following morning, but Carrie had no expectation of seeing him before a quarter-past, and it was nearly half-past ten before he appeared, blithely smiling and obviously happy to see her.

Carrie greeted him absently, because by then she had lost interest. She had seen Robert Sheraton and Sister Whitworth a few minutes before, and all thoughts of Ann, Phil and birthday presents had vanished. Consultant and midwife had entered the jewellers across the road—a jewellers, of all places! Surely they weren't buying an engagement ring? And where did that leave Mireille?

It wasn't possible; Mr Sheraton and Sister Whitworth weren't right for each other. Why, they were practically strangers! Three weeks wasn't a long enough acquaintance. They needed time to get to know each other, learn each other's tastes and interests, and. . . It wasn't fair!

Slowly the awful truth sank in. *She* fancied Robert Sheraton! Carrie's lips moved in a mute protest, then Phil's gusty sigh reminded her why she was in the High Street. She felt numb all over, and even when Phil tucked her small, mittened hand in his she felt nothing. People could die of shock. Not emotional shock, perhaps, but it was more serious than people realised.

'How are you, Carrie, love? I haven't seen you about lately,' Phil was saying, and a bemused Carrie turned her attention to her former boyfriend. By rights, she shouldn't be here, it was asking too much of her. And she didn't want to he here; she wanted to be strolling into the jewellers with Mr Sheraton.

'Oh, I'm fine. It's a bit cold for standing around, isn't it? You're half an hour late, Phil, and I'm on duty at twelve-thirty. Shall we get going?' Without waiting for

an answer, Carrie walked away, leaving the houseman
no option but to follow her.

All the while they were shopping, Carrie's thoughts
were on consultant and midwife. Jewellery was the
obvious choice for Ann's birthday but house doctors
never had money to burn, and Ann had tentatively
suggested an evening shawl. Debenhams had a good
selection, and Carrie determinedly turned Phil in that
direction. No way were they doing a tour of the jewellers!

Since Phil hated shopping, the purchase was soon
made—a pretty silver-threaded shawl. Then Carrie had
the bright idea of buying Ann an evening purse to match
the shawl. She had already bought a gynae textbook for
her. Not a wildly exciting present, but a necessary one.

Seeing Mr Sheraton and Sister Whitworth together
had taken away all her feeling of unease at meeting Phil
again. He was his usual supremely confident self, and
she studied him as they shared a very quick hamburger
lunch afterwards. He was really rather arrogant, if one
looked at him with eyes not clouded by love. One *could*
recover from a broken heart—hadn't she proved it twice
already?

'You're quite a girl, Carrie, love.' Phil smiled easily
across at her, and Carrie permitted herself a tight smile.
Suddenly she had outgrown Phil, and was grateful to
Ann for suggesting the outing. The scales had dropped
from her eyes, and she felt genuinely sorry for Phil, who
might never grow up. She wondered what he would be
like in twenty years, or ten years perhaps, when he was
the age that Mr Sheraton was now. . .

Carrie sighed without being aware of it. Mr Sheraton
was far too old for the likes of her, so it was just as well
it wasn't love she felt for him, wasn't it?

'Carrie?'

At last Phil's voice broke into Carrie's mournful
thoughts, and she said, 'Is it time to go?' She got up,
gathered up her shoulder-bag and basket then hurried
away. Work was the only cure. Work and studying. Yes,

she would throw herself into her studies and surprise everyone, including herself, she thought in wry amusement.

Phil caught her up and walked back with her to the hospital. They exchanged small talk, but to her embarrassment he kissed her on the mouth when they finally said goodbye. Not only were they on the hospital campus by then but it was past time for her to change into her uniform, and she struggled to free herself.

'I'll be late, Phil! For goodness' sake, let go!'

He grinned and drew her slight body more closely to him. 'That was for old times' sake, Carrie. See you!'

Despite her good intentions, Carrie was five minutes late on duty, and Sister Carter glared at her but made no comment. The comment would not be verbal, Carrie knew. Punishment would come in the form of duties normally carried out by the lowest grade of nurse on the ward, such as extra sluice duties or tidying the linen cupboard.

Marigold Ward was quiet as it wasn't an operating day and they hadn't been on emergency standby during the weekend, and Carrie busied herself getting the ward ready for visitors, once the lunches had been cleared away. But first she had to say hello to Doris Bramley, who had gone down for her op just before the weekend.

Mrs Bramley looked as troubled as ever, and confided to Carrie that she had been suffering a lot from wind. 'It's better now, Nurse, but it was chronic at first, that wind. Thought I was going off pop, I did!'

'You aren't experiencing any windy pains now, though?' Carrie asked. This wasn't an uncommon occurrence after surgery, but there appeared to be no abdominal distension, or any there had been had disappeared now.

'No, nothing like that now, Nurse. I'm on the mend, Sister says—but what about my husband? He wants to know——' Mrs Bramley broke off and reddened, then shrugged. 'I shouldn't be asking you young nurses but I

didn't like to ask Sister and I'd just die of embarrassment
if I had to ask that nice surgeon!'

'You mean about resuming normal marital relations
after the op?' Carrie asked briskly, and the patient
nodded. 'There's no reason to feel embarrassed about it,
Mrs Bramley. I'll ask Sister to come and have a word
with you, shall I? Or she'll see you in her office when
you're fit enough to walk that far. Would that be better?'

Often, patients didn't want to discuss their personal
problems in the ward itself, since the others in the
cubicle might hear, and Sister Carter was always willing
to talk to them in the office, and Carrie bustled away,
once she had received Mrs Bramley's permission to tell
Sister.

Since Mrs Bramley was 'her' patient, it was unfortunate that she had missed more than two days of the
woman's post-operative treatment, and she must catch
up on the condition of all the patients just as soon as she
had a moment. But first visitors, the VIPs.

Sister didn't insist on absolute tidyness except on
ward-round days, and, whatever her faults, Carrie
acknowledged that the Sister kept a happy ward. But
one person who wasn't happy on the ward was Ann
Haynes. She had given Carrie a strange look once or
twice and seemed offhand, but Carrie thought no more
of it until she went into the sluice a little later to test a
urine specimen.

Sluices and linen cupboards were time-honoured
places for nurses when they needed to cry, and the tears
were rolling slowly down Ann's cheeks when Carrie
bustled in.

'Hello, what's up? Not a lovers' tiff, surely?' Then
Carrie remembered that Ann couldn't have seen Phil
since the shopping expedition. 'Phil bought you a gorgeous shawl,' she went on, trying to cheer her friend up.

'And what did he buy you?' Ann demanded, wiping
her face on her apron.

When Carrie stared in surprise, Ann went on crossly, 'Don't stand there looking so innocent! You were seen!'

'See doing what?'

'Kissing *my* fiancé!' Ann said sharply, and Carrie groaned, while silently cursing Phil's stupidity.

'It was a kiss for old times' sake, Ann!' she insisted. 'That's what Phil said. He——'

'You'll be telling me next that Phil kissed *you*, instead of you kissing him! You flung your arms around his neck. The poor dear couldn't help himself!' Ann charged, while Carrie stared at her in dismay.

'Is that what Phil said? I'm surprised at him,' she said gently. She didn't want to hurt Ann's sensitive feelings and she tried to make allowances for the natural suspicions of a girl in love, but taking the blame for what happened was going too far.

'You were seen,' Ann emphasised. 'And from where the—the person was, you seemed to be taking the initiative. I thought you were my friend,' she went on woefully.

Carrie opened her mouth to demand the name of the person who had been spying on them, then a third person entered the argument. Robert Sheraton stood in the doorway of the sluice, eyeing them *and* the sluice with distaste, Steely eyes were fixed upon Carrie, and she tensed, wondering how much he had heard.

'If you young women haven't sufficient work to do, I'm sure Sister can find you something,' he said coldly.

'Sister's off duty now, sir,' Carrie said. Twin spots of colour burned in her cheeks as she prepared to do battle with him. Consultant or no consultant, he wasn't going to take out his evil temper on her! He could let fly at Mireille if he wanted someone to quarrel with.

There was no question of an altercation in the sluice, though, and when the surgeon beckoned Carrie's heart dropped like a stone. Anxiety replaced annoyance as she followed him meekly the whole length of the ward. Startled eyes marked their progress to the ward office, and the interesting turn of events would keep the women gossiping for hours. Carrie hoped they enjoyed the sight of her being led away in disgrace, for that, virtually, was what it was.

There was no one in the office, as far as she knew, the staff nurse being occupied behind a set of bed curtains, so at least there would be some privacy when she was ground into the dust.

Once in the office, Mr Sheraton waved a hand to indicate, presumably, that Carrie might sit, and she perched on the very edge of an uncomfortable chair which stood against the far wall. If he meant to sit behind Sister's desk he would have to swing his chair right around. Carrie intended to make it as awkward as possible for him, even though she knew she was behaving childishly. She could well imagine Aunt Moira's comments!

To her surprise, he lounged against Sister's desk, which meant that his rather large feet were only inches from her own. His black shoes were of soft, expensive-looking leather and Carrie wouldn't have been at all surprised to learn that they were handmade. She tried to concentrate on those shoes, and obstinately refused to raise her eyes. She only wished he would hurry up and get it over with—*she* had words to exchange with Ann Haynes!

'Isn't it rather greedy of you to steal that poor nurse's boyfriend?' Mr Sheraton asked quietly, and Carrie's head shot up.

'Greedy? He was mine first! Anyway, I didn't,' she went on. '*He* kissed *me*, and someone told Ann, only she assumed I was the one doing the kissing.' Green eyes sparking dangerously, she said quietly, 'I can't see what business it is of yours, sir—with respect,' she added grudgingly, and a faint smile touched the surgeon's mouth.

Carrie hurriedly glanced away. Concentrate on his feet, she told herself. You don't *want* to watch his mouth, or wonder what it would be like to be kissed by such a man.

'I'm glad it's with respect,' he said, his tone soft but no less dangerous, and she quaked inwardly. She had no business answering a consultant back. Well, all was lost now and Aunt Moira would be proved right, so she might as well satisfy her curiosity before she was asked to leave.

She raised her small face again, and was stunned to see that Mr Sheraton was actually smiling! A real smile this time, not the merest shadow that usually passed for one. She tore her eyes away from the pleasant sight, and stared straight through him. 'Are you going to marry Sister Whitworth, sir? I saw you going into the jewellers when I was waiting for Dr Mackie,' she hurried on, afraid lest he explode before she had finished.

'*Did* you?' The smile broadened and the consultant almost laughed. Carrie watched in amazement as the smile spread across his lean face. She liked the way his mouth curved, the light that sprang into those dark grey eyes, the cute little crows' feet at the corners of his eyes and mouth. He looked much younger, too. Almost in her own age-group, really, if one stretched it out a little.

Carrie smiled back, her eyes sparkling, but the sight didn't please Mr Sheraton, for his face settled again into its normal harsh planes, and she saw again the hard, ruthless man within. Just for a few seconds he had become human, and Carrie wondered what it would take to strip away the cold, autocratic barrier completely. Something perhaps that only Sister Whitworth could do.

'Sister Whitworth and I have known each other for a good many years,' he pointed out. 'We worked together at St Thomas's at one time,' he added, and Carrie brightened.

'You were buying her a birthday present!' she said happily, the problem solved.

Mr Sheraton choked, and she thought for a moment he was going to laugh again. 'I was not buying her a birthday present!' he said, in a strangled voice. 'Her birthday isn't until June.'

Carrie's lips had hardly formed themselves into an 'Oh!' when the telephone shrilled, and the moment for confidences was over.

Once she had dealt with the query, Carrie went out into the ward. There was work to be done. Staff Nurse would be wondering what had happened to her, and there were patients' teas to supervise, visitors to prepare for, and, most important of all, there were patients to talk to and comfort. Mr Robert Sheraton was ruthlessly pushed to the back of Student Nurse Caroline West's mind as she went about her duties. Occasionally, she imagined she saw his smile lingering in a corner of the ward or even in the sluice, but when that happened she plunged into her work with renewed vigour, and the smile faded.

CHAPTER FIVE

CARRIE saw nothing of the consultant for a day or two, and didn't know whether to be pleased or sorry. One thing made her happy, though—she and Ann were friends again, Ann having accepted that Phil's kiss had indeed been for old times' sake, and that the person who had seen them in town, a first-year student, had been exaggerating.

The ward remained busy, though, Carrie was glad. They were now full again, and it was obvious that Eileen Jordan would have to be discharged. She had made a good recovery but the family's housing problem remained acute, and this was causing Mrs Jordan distress. Gainsborough was a thriving market town but accommodation to let was in short supply, and house prices seemed to be going up all the time. Carrie was determined to have her own little place once she qualified but she knew she could never afford to live in Gainsborough. It might mean leaving St Hilda's, and she didn't think she could bear that.

There was a new student on the ward now, one straight from introductory block, and it was Carrie's job to take her around the ward, show her the different procedures, and generally make her feel welcome. Usually a staff nurse took newcomers in hand, but Sister Carter felt it better for a fellow learner to help at first, and Carrie felt proud that *she* had been chosen! The scatty Nurse West was maturing at last, she felt, and wished her aunt Moira could see her.

It would be nice, too, if Dad could see how well she was doing, Carrie thought wistfully, then shrugged away the thought as she turned to Nurse Brockway.

'You can help me with the vulval swabbing. That's for

Mrs Currie,' Carrie explained. 'You go and talk to her and try to explain what we're going to do. She knows anyway—I've just got to get something from the clinic.'

The junior scurried away while Carrie went into the clinic. The top shelf of the cupboard was high, and the backless chair didn't look all that safe but she hadn't time to seek out the steps. She was reaching over for a carton when some sound made her turn sharply, and she nearly overbalanced.

Strong arms caught her as she and the chair wobbled about, and, face flushed, Carrie began to thank her rescuer. Then piercing grey eyes caught her in their beam and she forgot what she was about to say.

For a moment, no, perhaps only half a second, Carrie thought she saw desire in their depths, but how could that be? Then the shutters came down again, Robert Sheraton released her, and she clung weakly to the high cupboard.

'Sister's on split duty today, sir. Staff Nurse is in charge—would you like me to find her?'

Even to her own ears, Carrie's voice sounded strange, totally unlike her usual cheery tones, and she hoped the surgeon wouldn't notice, or would put it down to fright because she had nearly fallen.

There was a moment of silence, which Carrie thought went on for hours, and she turned very carefully, only to see him shrug. 'No, don't bother, it's—personal,' he went on. 'Anyway, I have a Mrs Hyde coming in from the waiting-list.' He was speaking again, and Carrie collected her wayward thoughts, wondering what personal matter he had wanted to see Sister Carter about.

'We haven't a bed,' she pointed out, considering where they might put up a spare one. Mr Sheraton wouldn't try to admit a patient to an already full ward without good reason.

'Mrs Jordan will have to go,' he said flatly, and Carrie leapt to the defence of her favourite.

'She hasn't anywhere to go! You can't throw her out just like that!' she protested.

'I'm not throwing her out on to the streets, Nurse.' The surgeon spoke quietly but Carrie heard the edge in his voice. 'Mrs Hyde has a uterine prolapse,' he carried on, studying her as he spoke, his eyes narrowed. 'Hop down from that precarious chair and tell me what you know about that.'

He didn't offer to help her down, and Carrie thought perhaps that was just as well. She got down, then thought for a moment, before pouring out all she had learned from her gynae textbook.

'It's called procidentia,' she began. 'It's where some of the ligaments are weakened and the uterus comes down into the vagina.' She hesitated, wondering what else she could remember.

'What sort of symptoms might this lady report?' the surgeon prompted.

'Um. . .stress incontinence, I suppose. Yes, she would,' Carrie went on more confidently, 'and she would complain of—of, well, something coming down, or she might feel that she had a lump in her vagina. Oh, and she wouldn't be able to fully empty the bladder.'

'Yes.' The surgeon nodded. 'But procidentia is complete prolapse and this isn't common. What Mrs Hyde has is a partial prolapse, but it's causing her other symptoms as well, mainly mental ones. That's why I've decided to have her in,' he explained. 'You know something about it, anyway. Your textbook puts it admirably,' he added drily.

Carrie coloured. 'Yes, sir. It's got plenty of diagrams,' she muttered. 'I haven't actually seen a case yet, though,' she admitted, feeling that she ought to be honest with him.

'Firstly, Nurse West, I know your book has plenty of diagrams, because I wrote it,' the surgeon said pleasantly, moving towards Carrie as he spoke.

'Oh!' She backed away, feeling stupid because she hadn't known about the textbook.

'Secondly,' he went on inexorably, 'you do not see a "case", you see a patient. You mean you haven't yet nursed a *patient* with a complete prolapse, don't you, Nurse?'

By now, Carrie was backed up as far as she could go. Although he wasn't touching her, his face was only inches from her own, and she had time to admire his nice straight nose and dark eyes before, with a hearty sigh, he turned and walked out, leaving Carrie to recover in peace.

Feeling that her nerves wouldn't stand much more, she straightened her cap and marched out, intending to go back into the ward. She was just passing the office when the telephone rang, but it was Mr Sheraton who answered it, and Carrie hesitated for a moment before going into the office to prepare the folder for the new admission.

She checked to see that the necessary forms were inside. Putting the forms there was the job of the ward clerk, but they still had to be checked. There were Path Lab forms for routine blood tests, X-ray forms, weight charts. Now——

'What does my daughter want? Did she say?' The consultant's words at last penetrated Carrie's awareness, and she glanced over at him, her blood freezing. He was still on the phone, of course, and his remark hadn't been addressed to her, but—*daughter*?

'Tell her I'll be home in about an hour. I have a couple of patients to see first.' Mr Sheraton replaced the receiver, frowning, but before Carrie could say anything Sister Carter appeared in the doorway.

'Robert! Why wasn't I told you were here?' Then she saw Carrie, whose slight form had been hidden by the surgeon. 'I see Nurse is attending to your needs.' Sister's smile was barbed, but Carrie didn't intend to leave. She had a perfect right to be in the office.

'I'm getting the notes ready for the new admission, please, Sister,' she said crisply.

'New admission?' Sister turned puzzled eyes on the surgeon.

'I'm afraid so, Sister. A Mrs Brenda Hyde, uterine prolapse. I haven't quite decided on the op. She has problems,' the surgeon told her, with a charming smile.

Carrie watched as Sister's resentment visibly melted, and wondered if her senior knew the consultant had a daughter. And did he have a wife, as well? That was the important question!

She was still mulling over it as she carried on with her nursing duties. Mr Sheraton had a daughter. Was he a widower? Or divorced? Probably the latter, Carrie decided. Widowers were older men, surely? He wasn't all *that* old, probably in his mid-thirties.

No, Mrs Sheraton must still be alive. Probably they were estranged, since he was openly pursuing other women. There was still the mystery of his exact relationship with Sister Whitworth and what they were doing in the jewellers, and now he appeared to be courting Sister Carter again. And where did Mireille fit in? If he *was* still married, it was highly improper behaviour from a consultant and he ought to be struck off the register!

Still feeling indignant, though she could not have said why, Carrie went over to talk to Mrs Jordan, wondering where the surgeon intended sending her on discharge.

Eileen Jordan greeted her with a smile, as always, and Carrie patted her hand. 'Hello, again! I've come to talk to you; you always cheer me up,' she began, and Mrs Jordan chuckled.

She was sitting beside her bed, the inevitable knitting needles clicking away, but she set them aside as she greeted her favourite nurse. 'How are you, love? That sister not rushing you off your feet today, then?'

'No, we're slack, but we've a new lady coming in and I don't know where we're going to put her,' Carrie admitted, knowing she mustn't tell Mrs Jordan they were going to use *her* bed.

The woman shrugged. 'I dare say they'll be taking my bed, won't they? I've been wondering why they've not sent me home. I must be overdue for discharge, surely?' Her anxious brown eyes met Carrie's.

'Well—they're trying to find you somewhere to live, aren't they?' Carrie hedged. 'I know the social worker's been to see you.'

'Homes aren't that easy to find unless you can afford your own, duck, and we've never had the money. My husband was only on the land, you know. You can't save on a wage like that, and it wasn't as if we'd a tied cottage. We had a nice council flat at one time, but——' She stopped and appeared to be concentrating on her knitting, and Carrie put a sympathetic hand on her shoulder.

'Never mind, we'll think of something, Mrs Jordan. I expect Mr Sheraton will come up trumps!' she added hopefully, and the patient glanced up, her gaze shrewd.

'You young nurses fancy him, don't you? Well, I can't blame you. He's tall, dark and handsome, like some romantic hero, but there's more to him than that. He's got kind eyes. Have you noticed?'

Carrie hadn't. Whenever his eyes had been turned upon her, she had noticed how cold and steely they were, except during that brief moment in the clinic, and she supposed she must have imagined *that*. 'No, I hadn't noticed actually. The very next time he stares right through me, I'll tell him he's got kind eyes,' she promised, and Mrs Jordan smiled.

'Consultants do that, though, don't they? Stare right through learners, I mean. Still, it's only their way. They've got to keep a proper distance, I expect. Are you a knitter? There's a bit here I'm not sure about.'

Carrie obligingly bent her head and tried to sort out the knitting problem. Then, later, as she was mentally checking off her next chores, she saw a girl of about thirteen or fourteen hovering in the doorway.

She walked up the ward with her brisk nurse's walk, and smiled at the girl. 'I'm afraid it isn't visiting time yet, love. Is your mother a patient?' If she was a patient's child, the rules could be relaxed.

The tall girl shook her head, then brushed back a lock of heavy coal-black hair. 'No, I wanted to see my father. I don't feel very well,' she murmured.

Wondering if this was Mr Sheraton's daughter, Carrie took her by the arm. 'Come on, you can sit in the office. You look a bit flushed.' That was an understatement, and clearly the girl was in pain, biting her lip to keep from crying out. Carrie led her into the office, where Sister was just settling down behind her desk. She clicked her tongue in disapproval as Carrie seated the girl in the armchair. Then she, too, must have noticed the marked resemblance the girl bore to the consultant surgeon. She rose, all concern, but it was to Carrie that the girl spoke.

'I'm Ella, Mr Sheraton's daughter. He said he would be home soon, but the pain got worse and I thought I ought to come here,' she said, her voice scarcely audible. Then she doubled up with a little cry of pain, and Carrie hurried to fetch a kidney dish while Sister comforted Ella.

It might be acute appendicitis, Carrie decided, busily trying to diagnose the illness, since it was something quite common in teenagers and reminded her of her own appendicitis when she was about the same age. She put her cool hand on the girl's brow while she vomited, then covered the dish before whisking it to one side.

'There, is that better?' she spoke quietly, and the dark head nodded almost imperceptibly.

'Yes, thank you. I'm sorry to be a nuisance,' Ella Sheraton said politely, and Carrie frowned down at the bent head.

'No one thinks you're a nuisance. You've come to the

right place, anyway!' Carrie said cheerily, wondering whether the surgeon considered his daughter a nuisance. Well, shame on him if he did!

Sister, meanwhile, was ringing around trying to find Mr Sheraton, who wasn't carrying a bleep. 'Everywhere I try, he's either left or they're expecting him,' she grumbled. 'The man should have gone off duty by now.'

'If he had, this poor girl wouldn't still be suffering,' Carrie said crossly, forgetting the cardinal rule that one did not discuss patients in front of them. Forgetting also, in her annoyance, that the girl might well carry her words back to her father. By now, Mr Sheraton must have had more than enough of Nurse West's opinions!

Sister put out a call for him on the address system but without much hope, and the spasm had passed by the time he came hurrying in, his tie askew, his hair rumpled.

'What's all this then, Ella? A pain in the tum, um?' His tone was gentle, and, yes, his eyes *were* kind as he put a hand on his daughter's shoulder.

Ella nodded. 'Yes, Daddy, I'm sorry. I ought to have waited, you said you'd be home, but I couldn't!' The girl began to cry, almost silently, the way an adult might, and Carrie's heart melted. Always a kind-hearted girl, she cradled Ella's head to her apron and spoke soothingly.

Mr Sheraton stood back, then issued instructions to Sister Carter while Carrie gave his daughter tender loving care. 'They've a bed in the private wing,' he was saying. 'She can rest there, and we'll see what we can do.'

Carrie silently approved. The girl could rest in comparative peace and quiet there. She rather wished, though, that she could take Ella there herself. Someone in pain needed one particular person to cling to, but of course it wouldn't be allowed.

Ella wouldn't let go of Carrie's hand, though, and Mr Sheraton ordered her to accompany his daughter on the short journey to the private wing. Of course Carrie was delighted, but Mr Sheraton's autocratic demand that she drop everything else rankled later, when she had time to think about it.

The girl clung to Carrie's hand as she was taken up to the private floor, and Carrie could see the resemblance more clearly now. Ella hadn't her father's chilly grey eyes, but there was no doubt whose child she was. She had a smaller version of that sensuous lower lip, the same straight nose, long dark lashes, and that thick black hair.

Her big eyes met Carrie's bravely, though her voice trembled. 'I'm not going to die, am I, Nurse Carrie? Like Mother. *She* died during an operation.' Her voice trailed off when she mentioned her mother, and impulsively Carrie bent down and kissed her

Ella didn't want Carrie to leave her, but by the time she had been examined and a diagnosis of acute appendicitis made it was nearly ten o'clock and Carrie was on early duty the next day. Ella's operation was fixed for the following morning, and Carrie said gently, 'I have to go back to the nurses' home now, I'm on early shift tomorrow and I'll be on duty at half-past seven.'

'Is that before my op? Will you come to see me before I have it? Please?' Ella tugged at Carrie's fingers.

'Of course I will! I'll get up extra early and——' Carrie broke off as Mr Sheraton approached. 'I'll go now, but I'll come back tomorrow.' She rose from Ella's bed, and eyed the surgeon diffidently, wondering whether he would object. Not that it mattered; she would keep her promise to the girl, come what may.

Cool eyes met hers. 'You could spend the night in the wing, Nurse. Sister has a spare room, I'm sure. Ella will be glad of your company when she goes down to Theatre.' There was a half-smile on his face, but his tone brooked no argument and for once Carrie offered none.

'Yes, of course, sir,' she murmured obediently, and saw his eyebrows shoot up.

'My, my—you *have* become respectful.'

'Thank you, sir,' Carrie said with a saintly smile, 'I do try to be respectful.' The surgeon's barely suppressed chuckle followed her from the room. There was no doubt about it, she was making an impression on him. 'It's a pity it's the wrong impression,' she told herself, as she reached her tiny room and began to gather up her nightclothes and toilet things.

She took a final glance around the room, then saw the envelope on the floor. Puzzled, she picked it up. Someone must have pushed it under her door, and she hoped it wasn't a would-be suitor—she was definitely finished with men!

The note was from Terry, the medical student who had been the cause of her first argument with the consultant gynaecologist. Well, she certainly wasn't going out with him! It proved to be an invitation to a party the medical students were holding in the students' common room.

She treated herself to a sandwich and a cup of coffee in the almost empty canteen, then hurried back to Ella, who was lying awake but drowsy in a single room. A nurse sat by her bedside, reading, and Carrie exchanged a few words with her before smiling down at the patient.

Ella reached out for her hand and, comforted, drifted off to sleep without speaking. Carrie, wondering where Mr Sheraton was, sat there for a while then gently prised her hand away. She yawned as she left the room, intent on finding the night nurse. Tomorrow was going to be a very long day. 'Oh, sorry!' Carrie smiled an apology as she bumped into someone, then her smile faded as she saw it was Robert Sheraton.

He was casually dressed now, and her eyes widened as she took in the knife-creased fawn trousers and white polo-neck sweater. In his book 'casual' obviously meant neat and tidy, and almost as smart as 'formal'. He was freshly shaved, too, and his spicy aftershave drifted across to Carrie.

'Ella was asking for you, sir. I expect she was wonder-

ing what had happened to you,' Carrie said, not bothering to keep the reproach out of her voice. 'I'm glad
you've changed,' she hurried on before he could speak.
'You don't look so much like a surgeon in casuals. Ella
is uptight about having an op, you know.'

'She seems to have confided in you a great deal.' Mr
Sheraton's tone was cold, and Carrie resented it.

She drew herself up to her full five feet two and glared
at his chest, which was on a level with her eyes. Wishing
to be a few inches taller, she said pointedly, 'I'm not that
much older than Ella, and we have a lot in common. It's
natural she should talk to me.'

'Yes, I suppose that's true,' he agreed. 'You're nearer
to Ella's age than I am. Much nearer.'

Carrie glanced up to his face in time to see the tide of
sadness that swiftly passed over his handsome features.
Impulsively, she laid her small hand on his arm. 'Ella
loves you, I'm sure! But it's just that she needs another
girl—well, a woman—to talk to and——' She stopped,
her thoughts muddled. She felt she wasn't making much
sense, and if she carried on she might well hurt him. He
obviously cared about his daughter, even if he *was* a
workaholic. No doubt he would be in Theatre with her
tomorrow.

Gently he took her hand and squeezed it, while Carrie
stood, rooted to the spot. 'I *think* I follow your line of
reasoning, my dear. Thank you for taking care of Ella.'

Carrie watched his tall figure go into his daughter's
room, before making her own way to the small guest-
room she had been allocated.

She slept badly, her slumbers tormented by scenes of
Robert Sheraton smiling down at Sister Carter, and she
awoke with a sense of relief. At least the trauma of the
day could not be worse than that of the night.

CHAPTER SIX

CARRIE was allowed to give Ella her pre-med, and it was then that she saw the name on the record card: Mireille Maria Sheraton. *She* was the mysterious Mireille! Carrie felt almost light-headed with relief. She was still mulling over this when she took Mireille, or Ella, down to the private theatre suite.

Ella had tried to wring a promise from her that she would stay for the op, but permission had been refused by the consultant performing the operation, and Carrie wasn't sorry. Theatre work had never appealed to her, and seeing someone she had become fond of on the 'table' would have been upsetting.

That Mr Sheraton, a surgeon himself, might feel the same way had simply never occurred to her, and, when Ella was transferred first to the recovery room and later to her own bed, Carrie expected to see Mr Sheraton somewhere along the line. She made excuses for him at first, thinking he was busy with his patients and would come up immediately Ella came fully around.

She tended to the girl, once they were back in the small, impersonal room, overcome by sisterly feelings as she stroked that familiar black hair. Robert Sheraton had been paged, she knew, but he did not appear to be in the hospital. Surely he was interested in Ella's fate? He might have a chilly nature and ice-cold blood, but the man wasn't callous. Ella must mean something to him, surely?

Carrie got a shock when the surgeon strolled in nearly half an hour later. He had been riding! Her astonished gaze took in the well-fitted jacket, jodhpurs and riding boots, but before she could speak Ella burst into tears.

Father and daughter embraced, and Carrie left the

room, taking her surgical textbook with her. Glancing at her watch, she saw with surprise that it was nearly lunchtime. Had Mr Sheraton spent *all* morning riding?

She didn't know if she would be able to conceal her anger at his indifference. He could, at least, have gone on duty. If he needed to keep busy then the patients could have benefited. She could see that he would be anxious, but surely throwing himself into a hard morning's work was the best way to deal with that? Instead, he had chosen to spend the morning pleasing himself. Why, the man wasn't anxious and upset at all!

Carrie made an effort at studying, but her anger was so intense that she found it impossible to concentrate. She flicked through a few more pages without really seeing anything, hoping Mr Sheraton would soon go. Moments later, he left, without speaking to Carrie or even looking in her direction. No doubt he was ashamed. Well, he wasn't going to escape so easily!

'I have to find out when I'm to have my lunch break,' she told Ella gently when she returned to the room, to find Ella much brighter and clearly delighted with her father's visit.

'Why do you want a break? Can't they give you something on a tray? I want you here,' Ella said plaintively, but Carrie shook her head.

'You won't feel like eating, and you might be sick if I had my lunch in here. I'll just ask Sister—shan't be long.' Carrie hurried away before Ella could protest further, then set off in pursuit of the surgeon.

She spotted Mr Sheraton striding across the car park towards his car, and she broke into a run. He wasn't going to get away without a few well-chosen words from Student Nurse Caroline West! It would probably be *ex*-Student Nurse West after this but, for Ella's sake, she had to point out the error of his ways.

It was terrible, loving a person then finding out that he or she wasn't the slightest bit interested in you. Ella must be dreadfully upset, even though she didn't show it. When you loved someone, you——

Carrie ground to a halt, her eyes widening in horror. Just then Mr Sheraton turned and waited. Robert Sheraton was waiting for her, but not in the way she hoped. It was crazy, absolutely crazy, but she was falling in love with Ella's father!

As if in a dream, Carrie resumed her brisk stride towards the man who saw her only as a temporary companion for his daughter.

'Don't rush, Nurse West. You'll have another of those hot flushes!'

Carrie tried hard not to laugh, but in the end the laughter won and the consultant joined in. 'I'm sorry, it isn't fair to tease you,' he said after a moment. 'Ella blushes easily as well.'

That gave Carrie the opening she needed, and her laughter faded. She couldn't find it in her heart to be angry with him. Not now that she had discovered this shameful love for him. She mustn't hurt him—yet he did not hesitate to hurt Ella, the child he presumably loved. She took a deep breath, wondering whether she would find the courage to speak out.

'Ella was wondering where you were.' Carrie kept the reproach out of her voice—just—but the surgeon wasn't fooled.

'Was it Ella, or little Nurse West, I wonder?' There was pain in his dark eyes, and Carrie bit her lip.

'I didn't mean——' she began, but he wouldn't let her finish.

'I stayed on in the waiting-room until I heard that Ella was all right, then I went riding because I needed to get away,' Robert Sheraton said gruffly. He cleared his throat before continuing, and Carrie realised he was deeply upset. The pain was still in his eyes. 'Ella's mother died in Theatre, Carrie. Cowardly though it may seem, I couldn't face seeing my daughter on the operating table. Perhaps it isn't possible for you to understand that,' he added, with a curiously dejected shrug, and Carrie wanted to cry.

He did care about Ella, after all! He wasn't the man of stone she had believed him to be. She opened her mouth to reassure him, but the words wouldn't come at first, then she managed, 'I *do* understand! Really I do! I——' She so desperately wanted to offer him tender loving care, put out her hand and touch him, let him feel the sympathy flowing from her, but she mustn't. Then throwing caution to the winds, she did put out her hand, resting it on his arm for a moment. 'I'm sorry. I did know about your—your wife,' she said, almost choking on the word, 'but I didn't think——' No, that was the trouble, she never thought. It simply hadn't occurred to her that a surgeon might not be able to face an operation when the patient on the table was his own dearly loved daughter.

'Never mind, Carrie. Thank you for taking care of Ella,' he said gently, then took her hand and squeezed it. The firm pressure of his fingers was almost more than Carrie could bear, but she summoned up her usual cheery smile.

She made no attempt to pull her hand free from his grasp, and the surgeon looked down at their clasped hands, frowning, as if he didn't know how they came to be holding hands.

'I'd better go,' he said shortly, releasing her, and getting into his car.

Carrie didn't linger. Overcome by this new and wonderful knowledge, she almost ran back to the private wing, her heart singing. He loved his daughter, and he had loved his wife. And I love him, she reflected wistfully, a strictly forbidden love. Life was too cruel sometimes.

After lunch, Carrie was told to report to her own ward, and she met Mrs Hyde, the new patient. The particular nurse allocated to Brenda Hyde was Ann Haynes and there was little Carrie could do for the

woman except when Ann was off duty. The ward was
busy and they were glad to see her back, so it was nearly
finishing time before she had a chance for a talk with
Mrs Hyde.

Apart from her prolapse, Mrs Hyde had problems of
a psychiatric nature. Carrie hadn't yet nursed someone
like that, and was a little wary at first. Mrs Hyde had a
history of admissions to mental hospitals, and suffered
from quite severe depression at times. An additional
trauma, such as an operation, might alter the delicate
balance in her mind, but her symptoms were now so
distressing that Mr Sheraton and her psychiatrist had
thought the risk worth taking.

It was a salutary lesson to Carrie to know that the
patient was just as wary of general nurses as they were of
her, and in her usual forthright manner she tried to
make Mrs Hyde feel welcome, having no doubt that Ann
would have difficulty in relating to her.

'I'm Carrie—Nurse West. I've just started my second
year, Mrs Hyde. Is there anything I can do for you?'
Carrie began, wondering whether she would get any
response.

Brenda Hyde was forty-nine but looked younger than
her age, and shrewd hazel eyes gazed at Carrie for an
instant, then she smiled diffidently.

'No. I don't think so, duck. Look.' She held out the
photograph she had been holding, and Carrie took it,
beginning to relax.

'He's my youngest daughter's boy, dear. He's nearly a
year old, and he's a lovely little soul, if I *do* say so! They
had it taken a couple of days ago, so's I'd have it to
comfort me.' Her voice faltered a little, and Carrie
squeezed her hand, before duly admiring the picture of
a terribly overweight baby.

'It's a pity he's too young to visit you,' Carrie commented. 'Are your children coming to see you later?'

The patient's worry lines deepened, and her eyes grew
bright with unshed tears. 'No, only the baby's mother,

my Jean. Me and my son's wife don't get on. She's too good for the likes of me, or so she thinks.' This was said with such bitterness that Carrie didn't know what to say for a moment. Having no experience of psychiatric nursing as yet, she was afraid of making matters worse.

Then Mrs Hyde swallowed her tears. 'Don't mind me, Nurse—Carrie, did you say your name was? Nice name, that.'

'It's short for Caroline, but my aunt is the only person who calls me that. I'm nothing like a Caroline!' Carrie confessed, and was rewarded by a thin smile.

'I go down for my op tomorrow, they tell me,' Mrs Hyde went on slowly. 'That Nurse Haynes, she hasn't got your cheery smile, dear. Will I be all right?'

Carrie gave her the benefit of that cheery smile. 'Don't worry, Mrs Hyde. I know everyone says that, but really you'll be fine. Mr Sheraton's a wonderful surgeon,' she assured her.

Mrs Hyde nodded, then said, 'It's a long time since I was in hospital. General hospital, that is. I've been in that old mental hospital what's just closed down, but last time I went to some posh place. A new clinic, it was, in a lovely old house in the country. They called the psychiatrist "the Buccaneer"!' she went on. 'He was a love, very kind.'

'So is Mr Sheraton, though I wouldn't call him a buccaneer!' Carrie said, chuckling at the thought. 'Keep smiling though, that's what my old tutor used to say when everything got us down.'

Carrie felt that she hadn't been of much help to the patient, but promised to get the staff nurse to see her about the operation itself. Mrs Hyde seemed to know roughly how long she would be in but had either forgotten or not been told details about the op, and Carrie didn't like to interfere, bearing in mind Mr Sheraton's remarks.

Only Sister Carter was in the office when Carrie went

in search of the staff nurse, and when she told Sister about Mrs Hyde Sister looked at her in surprise.

'I should have thought *you* would fill in the details, Nurse West. After all, you're in well with the consultant gynaecologist,' she almost snapped.

Carrie gasped. 'That's unfair, Sister! Mr Sheraton asked me to stay with his daughter! I couldn't say no, could I? Anyway, Mrs Hyde isn't my patient. Ann Haynes is looking after her interests, and I can't interfere, surely?' With an effort, Carrie struggled to keep the resentment out of her voice. In well with the consultant gynaecologist, indeed! If only she were!

'It seems as though Nurse Haynes hasn't been performing her duties adequately, then,' Sister commented, getting to her feet. 'I'll have a word with Mrs Hyde. In the meantime, read her case notes, and make sure you understand the type of depression she's suffering from, as well as the op she's in for, and the probable prognosis. Oh, and the medication.'

Sister sailed out of the office before a horrified Carrie could protest. Now there would be trouble for Ann, and it was all *her* fault. She knew Ann had gone off duty a few minutes early, and if Sister found out it would mean even more trouble for Carrie's sensitive friend.

Mr Sheraton was with Ella when Carrie popped in after duty. Curiously shy for once, she stammered and blushed, and stayed only a few minutes. Her forbidden love made her feel self-conscious, and she was afraid the surgeon's X-ray eyes would see into her heart. How he and Sister Whitworth would laugh! Well, no, Sister Whitworth wouldn't, Carrie acknowledged. The midwifery sister was a dear, and if the surgeon was able to win her love he was a lucky man indeed. Carrie considered the jolly, popular sister to be far too good for the man. Sister Carter, now—that would teach him a lesson!

He was in his working clothes. In his case, these consisted of a charcoal-grey suit with a waistcoat, and a pristine white shirt and sober tie. Plus the handmade gleaming black shoes, of course. Carrie tried hard not to look at him, and since Ella was the one she had come to see there was no reason to talk to the consultant, beyond acknowledging his brief greeting.

It was difficult to shake off the impression that he was watching her, though. He ought to be looking at his daughter, but Carrie could feel his intense gaze upon her, and it made her even more self-conscious. So much so that as she thankfully made her escape she turned too quickly and knocked a book off Ella's locker.

Moving more quickly than she would have believed possible, the surgeon caught the book before it fell, then turned those mesmerising eyes upon Carrie. 'Are you all right, Nurse?'

'Mm, yes, fine, thank you,' she muttered in confusion. Eyes bright and face very pink, she edged out of the room, after Ella had extracted a promise from her to visit every day.

'Stay a *long* time when you come, Carrie,' she called plaintively, as Carrie made her escape.

Then she heard Mr Sheraton's voice. 'Nurse has her own life, Ella. She can't be at our beck and call every day. She has to study as well, you know.'

'But I need her!' Ella's voice rose in a wail, and Carrie was glad she wasn't the girl's private nurse. Ella showed signs of becoming a girl for whom other people hurried to sweep away obstacles. She really needed a mother, and Sister Whitworth would fit the bill admirably, Carrie decided as she trudged up the stairs to her spartan little room. *She* certainly could not be expected to mother the girl. A stepmother only seven years older than the stepdaughter was out of the question. Laughable, really.

Feeling the tears begin to well up, Carrie slammed her door, but it did nothing to help heal her broken heart.

Ann was on late duty the following morning, so it fell to Carrie to accompany Mrs Hyde when the porters called to take her for surgery. She was conscious and not as

drowsy as Carrie would have wished. The pre-med
sometimes had the unfortunate effect, on certain individ-
uals, of making them more alert rather than sleepy. She
would have to mention that once they were in the ante-
room where the anaesthetic was administered.

Carrie delivered her patient and the message, then
walked quickly back to Marigold, her thoughts on the
tall lean figure she had glimpsed in Theatre. Even in
theatre greens and mask she had recognised Mr
Sheraton, his tall figure dwarfing that of Mr
Cunningham.

If Carrie was rather abstracted for the rest of the
morning, no one commented on it, not even Sister
Carter. Carrie wondered if she, too, spared the time to
dwell upon the surgeon and his life-saving work. Probably not, she conceded. By the time one reached the
heights of ward sister, one would take a surgeon's
dedication for granted.

But I shan't, she thought. Shaking her head firmly
and having to suffer an old-fashioned look from one of
the patients, Carrie blushed, then went about her work,
putting surgeons, dedicated or otherwise, firmly out of
her mind.

Two other patients were going down for surgery as
well as Mrs Hyde, so it was a busy morning and Carrie
had no time to dwell upon the interesting fact that she
had fallen in love with the consultant gynaecologist. How
Judy would chuckle if she knew! But Judy must never
know.

Doris Bramley greeted her as an old friend. She was
up and about now, and was sitting in the dayroom when
Carrie popped her head around the door just before
lunch.

'Everything all right, Mrs Bramley? No problems?'
There wasn't really time to sit down but Carrie perched
on the arm of Mrs Bramley's chair.

'Not now I've seen you, Nurse Carrie. Your smile
always makes me feel better,' Mrs Bramley confided,

then reached into the bag by her side. 'Here, I got my hubby to bring in a box of chocolates for you, but you've been that busy all morning I haven't liked to stop you.' She held out a small box of milk chocolates. 'I know you girls are always eating!'

'I'm afraid you're right. Thank you!'

A delighted Carrie took the box to the office to share with her colleagues. Patients were awfully kind on gynae wards, always giving the nurses sweets or biscuits, and once a patient had given her a plant.

Feeling more at peace with the world, Carrie went to her lunch and when she returned Ann was back on Marigold. Carrie wondered uneasily if Sister had said anything to her about Mrs Hyde and not keeping her fully informed, but dismissed the thought after a moment. Sister was far too busy on an ops day to even remember their conversation of the previous afternoon.

But she had underestimated Sister Carter, who was unlikely to forgo an opportunity to tell Ann off, and her friend was weeping in the linen cupboard when Carrie came upon her unexpectedly.

At first she didn't see Ann, who was trying to hide by burying her head, ostrich-like, in a pile of pillows.

When Ann looked round and saw Carrie, she burst into a fresh crop of tears.

'Look,' Carrie began, 'I'm sorry if Sister has been on to you, but I really didn't mean to——'

'Didn't you? I think you are the most jealous, spiteful girl I know!' Ann howled. 'And I thought you were my friend!'

Taken aback, Carrie could do no more than watch as Ann's tears dried at last. 'You deliberately set out to get me into trouble!' Ann charged. 'It's because of Phil. Don't think I don't know! You wanted him for yourself!'

'I *did* know him before you,' Carrie pointed out, her voice chilly. 'We went around for weeks before he suddenly dropped me, but I don't bear you a grudge for that!'

'Oh? You're telling me you've got someone else?'
Ann's voice was full of hope, but the 'someone else'
Carrie was pining for would not do at all!

'Well, no, I haven't, but——'

'There you are, then! Just because you and Phil were
—were *lovers* before, it doesn't mean he wants you
back!'

Carrie's eyes grew bigger and rounder at the enormity
of the lie Phil must have spun her. 'But we weren't
lovers! Oh, Ann, Phil didn't say that, did he?' Carrie
had to resist the urge to shake her. Of all the addle-
brained fools, Ann Haynes took the prize! Of course, if
Phil *had* let her believe that, Ann couldn't really be
blamed, she supposed.

'Oh, Carrie, I'm sorry!' Ann said unexpectedly. 'I
didn't mean those hateful things I said. It's just that
you're so pretty and—and I'm not sure if Phil really
loves me. I know you went out with him for ages and I
keep wondering why he turned to me.'

Carrie had spent much of her time wondering the
same thing, but didn't say so. 'If Phil doesn't love you,
that's hardly *my* fault, Ann. He certainly doesn't love
me,' she said.

Mr Sheraton was in the ward office as Carrie stalked
out of the cupboard, her arms piled high with sheets,
and his gaze was cold as she passed the open door. He
had clearly just come from Theatre, but could he have
heard the altercation? No, Carrie shook her head, then
dropped a sheet. Muttering crossly as she picked it up,
she still wondered uneasily whether he might have heard
something. He had to pass that way to get to the office
and he certainly hadn't been on the ward when she had
gone in search of linen. If he *had* heard, Ann's words
would have destroyed what little chance she had with
him.

Before she went back to the nurses' home to change,
Carrie intended popping in to see Ella. Tonight was the
medical students' party and she fully intended going,

despite her earlier decision not to. After Ann's remark, which Mr Sheraton *might* have overheard, he would think the worst of her anyhow, so what did it matter where she went? It might be rather fun and she was sorely in need of someone bestowing a sunny smile on *her*, for a change.

Ella met her with a cross face and a demand that she spend the entire evening with her.

'I'm sorry, love, but I do have a full-time job. Being a nurse isn't one long holiday,' Carrie pointed out firmly, and Ella nodded.

'I'm sorry, Nurse Carrie. Not that it mattered, anyway; Sister Whitworth came in to see me!' Ella brightened up, and she surveyed Carrie through half-closed black lashes.

'I'm glad! She's lovely, isn't she?' Carrie forced enthusiasm into her voice. The sooner Sister married Mr Sheraton, the better as far as Ella was concerned. 'Has your father got a housekeeper?' she asked idly, and Ella was clearly surprised.

'Oh, yes, and we've got a——' She stopped, her gaze going to the half-open door. Her father stood there, a faint smile playing around that firm, sensuous mouth.

Carrie wrenched her eyes away quickly, afraid lest he sense her love for him. She got up. 'I was just going, sir,' she murmured, studiously avoiding his gaze.

'Don't let me chase you away, Nurse West,' he said formally, settling himself on the edge of his daughter's bed and smiling at them both.

'Why don't you call her Carrie, Daddy? You did before.' Ella's remark made Carrie feel hot and bothered, and she began to make excuses to leave.

'I have to shower and change now, sir. Then I've some studying——' she began, but Ella chipped in importantly,

'*I* know where she's going! To the medical students' party! I wish I could go,' she added plaintively.

Carrie could feel the disapproval emanating from the

surgeon's every pore, and silently cursed her own stupidity in telling Ella. She'd thought it would be of interest
to the girl, relieve the boredom a bit. She had even
discussed what she was going to wear—a brilliant saffron
dress, in a filmy floating fabric. It was far too good for a
students' party, but there were so few occasions for
dressing up at St Hilda's that nurses tended to wear
exotic creations even for informal dances. It was a dress
that her sister had sent, and Carrie hadn't had a chance
to wear it before. Of course Mr Sheraton would probably
feel she was out to snare one of his students, but she
couldn't help wishing that *he* could see her in all her
finery. He had seen her only in her uniform, and in the
mountains of woollies she had worn at her uncle's.

'You're having very cross thoughts, Carrie. May we
join in?' Mr Sheraton asked drily, and Ella giggled.

Carrie hesitated, torn two ways. There was that little
smile again, and she wanted to wipe it from his face,
yet. . . He had called her 'Carrie'. As she struggled to
find some polite rejoinder, his smile became a laugh, and
both girls looked their surprise.

'You would be good for Daddy if he wasn't so old,'
Ella observed with a bright smile. There was a strained
silence for a moment and Carrie didn't know what to
say.

'Am I old?' Mr Sheraton turned to his daughter, who
nodded emphatically.

'Yes, you are rather, you know, and it's such a pity.
Carrie makes you laugh,' she added, her tone so wistful
that Carrie's heart was wrung.

'I'd better go,' she muttered. Impulsively, she went
over to Ella's bed and kissed her. 'I'll tell you all about
the party tomorrow,' she promised, then made her
escape.

The girl needed a *father*, not only a mother. He
neglected her emotionally, and Carrie's heart bled for
her, reminding her in some degree of her own home life.
Like Ella, she really had no one, except Judy, of course.

Judy. In all the trauma, Carrie had almost forgotten her beautiful and talented sister. Yes, Judy ought to be down here by now, but with Judy one never quite knew when to expect her. She and Dad were alike in that respect. Carrie sighed, but didn't know why she did so.

CHAPTER SEVEN

NEXT day, Carrie had just a morning to work then was due for some time off—time she really felt she should spend with Uncle Charles and his wife. And, of course, Judy, for she had finally arrived at their uncle's while Carrie was at the noisy and disappointing party.

Much as she wanted to see her sister again, the prospect of a prolonged visit to Aunt Moira did not appeal, and Carrie felt disloyal about her lack of enthusiasm. Then, too, their father might put in an appearance, and she would once more be the ordinary little daughter that he found so difficult to understand and impossible to love.

As promised, she paid a quick visit to Ella when she went off duty, to cheer herself up as much as to cheer Ella, who was bubbling over because she was leaving hospital. 'Guess what, Carrie? I'm to have some convalescence—and you're to take care of me!' She sank back against the pillows, face flushed.

'Where? Will you go on holiday?' Carrie asked in surprise.

'Oh, I don't know. I'll probably go to my great-aunt Aggie's. It doesn't matter, as long as I get out of this dreary hole!'

Carrie wagged a finger at her. 'That's no way to speak of good old St Hilda's! They saved your life, you know,' she said gently, and Ella pouted.

'Yes, so they did. Anyway, Daddy said I must have a nurse to look after me, just for a few days, and I chose you. Oh, Carrie, we'll have such fun!' She clapped her hands together like a small child, and Carrie impulsively hugged her. In many ways, Ella was young for her years. Carrie decided that seeking a mother's love in every woman she met accounted for her sometimes infantile behaviour.

It appeared that Ella had read her mind. 'Sometimes I wish I had a mother, then I wouldn't need to ask people favours,' she said simply. 'Though of course Daddy will *pay* you.' She seized Carrie's hand. 'He wouldn't expect you to work for nothing. He's really rather rich,' she went on, with a giggle.

'I'm sure Mr Sheraton knows that I can't stay with you, pet,' Carrie said gently. 'I'm a learner. That means I can't take much time off without being penalised. I have to do a certain number of days' training,' she went on, seeing that Ella didn't understand.

'Oh, you can catch up, or put back your exams, can't you?'

'I don't *want* to put back my exams!' Carrie was exasperated. 'Three years is long enough as it is!'

Ella's face crumpled, and sobs racked her skinny body. Carrie felt dreadful, worse than a criminal. They were comforting each other when Mr Sheraton walked into the room, and Carrie sprang up in confusion. Now he would be angry and he had every right to be. No! He had no right to promise Ella something that he must know was impossible! 'Mr Sheraton——' she began, but Ella forestalled her.

'I told Carrie she was going to look after me, but she said she won't!' Ella said pathetically, as she held out her arms to her father.

He crossed swiftly to the bed and took his daughter's hands in his large, strong ones. 'What have I told you about asking people favours?'

'It wasn't really a favour, Daddy. I said you would pay her! You will, won't you?' Ella went on eagerly, and Carrie found herself crumpling her thick uniform dress in her agitation. And it creased so easily, too. Of course she wanted to help Ella, wanted to be near Ella's father as well! It was out of the question, though. She hadn't any leave due till Easter.

'Nurse West is not going to be at your beck and call, young lady, and she is *not* going to look after you.' The consultant's voice was firm and brooked no argument.

Carrie heard him in silence, but Ella wailed, 'Daddy I must have Carrie! We could have *fun* together.'

Mr Sheraton shook his head. 'It's all arranged, my pet. Sister Whitworth has agreed to stay for a few days.'

Ella digested this information in stunned silence, as did Carrie. Sister Whitworth! It was only to be expected, really. Peg Whitworth would keep Ella under control. Yet the girl needed someone younger, to have fun with, as she said.

Carrie felt Mr Sheraton's eyes upon her, and she knew she was expected to uphold his authority. Pinning a bright smile to her face and hoping her expression didn't give her away, she assured Ella that it would be for the best. 'Sister Whitworth's great fun. We all like her, you know.'

'Yes, Daddy and I knew her before we came here,' Ella admitted. 'She's very kind, I suppose—but I wanted you, Carrie!' Clearly Ella didn't intend to give in without a fight.

'I'm sure we can arrange for Nurse West to visit during your convalescence,' the surgeon said smoothly. 'If that wouldn't be a burden to you, Nurse?'

He turned to Carrie and smiled, that gentle, charming smile, and at that moment she would have done *anything* for him! A smile, and just for her alone.

Having assured them that she would be delighted to call to see Ella whenever possible, Carrie was at last free to leave. Ella would be discharged home while she was off duty, and that was probably just as well.

She wondered later what the surgeon's home would be like. Some mansion, probably. Their orthopaedic consulant lived in a five-bedroomed mock-Georgian-style house in the country, yet somehow Carrie couldn't picture Robert Sheraton in such opulent surroundings. She supposed, if she thought about it at all, that he *looked* wealthy, with his handmade shoes and expensive suits, but there was nothing ostentatious about him. He had a fearfully expensive car, but it wasn't brand new. He——

'Ah Carrie!'

She whirled round, her mouth half opening in surprise at seeing the consultant, as though her mind had conveniently conjured him up at the flick of a switch. She clutched her overnight case to her as if to ward him off, though that was the last thing she wanted to do!

It was beginning to rain, a fine rain which came at her almost horizontally, the capricious wind tugging at her hair and clothing. It would, just when she wanted to present a neat and tidy appearance to her uncle and aunt, not to mention a certain consultant surgeon. The certain consultant surgeon's expression was disapproving, and Carrie winced.

'Haven't you the sense to wrap up warmly?' he snapped, unreasonably she felt, since she was wearing four jumpers. 'Where's your umbrella?'

'It's too windy and I left it at——' she began, but he left her no time to finish.

'You've no more sense than Ella sometimes. Come along, I've no time to stand here arguing with young girls.'

Carrie gasped, but before she could rally herself he took her by the hand and urged her towards the warmth of his car. Realising at last that she was to be given a lift to her uncle's home, she stopped struggling and settled thankfully into the seat.

'This is luxury, you know.' She snuggled down beside him, and he shot her a grim smile.

'If you want a car like this, you had better marry a consultant when you're older,' he remarked, as he drove out of the big iron gates, leaving St Hilda's ancient grey buildings behind them.

Carrie's smile was twisted. 'Consultants don't notice student nurses in *that* way,' she remarked, pretending to be absorbed in the view. The fact that rain was obscuring her vision was irrelevant. 'Some of them are too proud to even speak to us,' she went on, pointedly.

'I'm not proud, Carrie.' His voice was gentle, and, wonderingly, Carrie half turned in her seat.

He was concentrating on the road and couldn't see the loving expression in her eyes. Which was just as well, she acknowledged. With a faint smile, she settled back in her seat to enjoy the short journey, and it wasn't until they left the town behind that she realised—this wasn't the road to Uncle Charles's house!

'We've gone too far!' she protested, tugging at Robert Sheraton's sleeve.

'We're never likely to do that,' was his cryptic reply. 'I thought you might like a bite to eat before you wend your way home to your uncle Charles. *Is* that your home, by the way? You mentioned your sister but isn't there anyone else?'

Carrie shook her head, the foxy hair flying in all directions. 'No, well, only my father, but Judy's *his* favourite and I don't really fit into his world,' she confessed. 'He rents a flat in London but he's got a house in the country for weekends, near Chipstead, in horsy country.' She hesitated, aware that her remarks might be misconstrued. 'The people he mixes with, they aren't *my* kind of people,' she finished. 'You know, they're always throwing lavish parties and—and mixing with the upper classes.' She waved a hand airily, and was disconcerted to hear his soft chuckle, and she reddened. Well, of course *he* was that sort of person, wasn't he? Not her sort at all. Then his earlier remark finally sank in, and she turned her head, regarding him out of wide green eyes. 'I *am* rather hungry, now you mention it,' she said pertly, and he laughed outright.

'I've never known a nurse who wasn't!' he said lightly, quite spoiling his invitation. 'We'll stop somewhere and you can eat to your heart's content. But perhaps you

would rather I dropped you off for a Big Mac or
something like that? That's the sort of place Ella likes.'

'I'm not Ella's age, Mr Sheraton, I'm a woman of
twenty,' Carrie said firmly, daring him to laugh.

'Of course. I apologise, Nurse West.' There was a hint
of amusement in his voice but Carrie chose to ignore it.
Then he went on, in a thoughtful voice, 'I really *do*
apologise. Of course you aren't a child, far from it. I
ought to have realised.

Carrie wondered what it was he ought to have realised,
but Robert Sheraton didn't choose to explain.

'Enjoying yourself, Carrie?' Mr Sheraton's voice was
light, teasing, but his gaze was unfathomable, and Carrie
gave him a shy smile that was curiously unlike her.

'Yes, thank you very much,' she said politely, and his
smile was wry.

'You sounded like Ella then,' he commented. 'And,
just like Ella, I suppose you want a sweet, gooey
pudding?'

Carrie considered the suggestion, her head on one
side, the bright, wayward curls dancing a little as she
moved her head. Being likened, yet again, to his ado-
lescent daughter didn't at all please her. She wanted him
to think her elegant, sophisticated, worldly, experi-
enced. . . She emitted a faint sigh. 'I'd rather like an ice,
if that's all right?'

The ice was procured, though she noticed he didn't
have one himself. The meal had been superb, a rich
creamy soup followed by chicken in a tarragon-flavoured
sauce. Carrie knew she wouldn't get anything like that
at her uncle's.

'I suppose you have your dinner at night?' she asked
suddenly, wanting to prolong the time she could spend
with him. 'I mean, I like this sort of thing, but I expect
you have steak and things at night,' she went on aim-
lessly, aware that he was watching her in some amuse-

ment. That was all she was good for, a laugh for the surgeon!

'I don't eat red meat, Carrie, just chicken and fish. I really prefer vegetarian dishes, though I'm *not* a vegetarian,' he admitted.

'Judy's a vegetarian!' Carrie blurted out before she thought better of the idea. 'At least I think she is. She's always talking about it.' Judy spent a lot of time talking, making grandiose plans, but had probably changed her mind a long time since.

'Tell me about Judy.' Mr Sheraton leaned towards her across the restaurant table, and Carrie decided she wasn't enjoying the vanilla ice, after all. She caught a tantalising whiff of his after-shave, and could feel herself colouring as he surveyed her. If only he wouldn't look at her like that! As if. . . As if he cared for her but was afraid she might bite. . .

'Well,' she began, reluctant to discuss her beautiful sister, 'she's pretty and—and a bit older than me. And she writes books—I told you that, didn't I?'

'What sort of books? Romantic tales, that sort of thing, I suppose?'

Mr Sheraton didn't sound that interested, and Carrie murmured something that he could take as 'Yes, that sort of thing', if he wished. She didn't like to tell him Judy wrote horror novels, quite sucessful ones. It didn't sound at all romantic. 'She's very successful,' Carrie said instead, and Mr Sheraton raised a brow, her wide eyes following the movement.

'Yes, you told me that. But she doesn't write for a living, surely? Doesn't she do something useful with her life?'

He sounded faintly disapproving and Carrie brightened. 'She used to work at St Hilda's. She was in the office for a while. She tried nursing but she didn't like it.' Since Judy had given nursing only a three-week trial, Carrie often thought Judy might have liked it very well if she had persevered. Not to like nursing was something she couldn't understand.

'Your sister probably didn't give it a fair chance.' The consultant dismissed Carrie's talented sister, then leaned towards her, his eyes kind. 'And what about you? What made you take up nursing?'

Taken aback, Carrie almost stammered, 'Well, I—I suppose I've *always* wanted to be a nurse. I used to bandage my dolls, and give them medicine. And my mother had MS. I only vaguely remember her, but I suppose her condition must have influenced my decision to take up nursing.'

She had never considered any other career. True, she sometimes regretted it, hated the long and unsocial hours, but the compensations far outweighed the disadvantages. 'My father says I'm a natural nurse,' she said instead, suddenly remembering his words.

'That's the greatest compliment anyone can pay a nurse, Carrie,' Robert said gently. 'It's something you can go back to, if you leave to start a family.'

Carrie's eyes widened, then she blushed. Yes, she *would* like to start a family—with the man himself! 'Yes, I expect you're right,' she muttered. 'What about you? Does surgery run in your family?'

A faint smile crossed the surgeon's face. 'Side-stepping personal questions, Carrie? No, my father was an accountant and no one in the family had even thought about a medical career.' He paused. 'I thought perhaps Ella might follow in my footsteps but she hates the very idea of healing the sick, tending the halt and the lame.'

'I'm sorry, really I am,' Carrie put in, wishing she could offer him more comfort. 'I expect you wanted a son, but you could still have one, couldn't you? I mean——' She stopped, aghast at what she had said.

There was an ominous silence, then Robert Sheraton's lips quivered as though he was biting back a laugh. 'Yes, that's true. I'm not too old to become a mother, am I?'

'Oh, you!' Carrie exclaimed, then grinned at him.

'You cheer me up, Carrie. Thank you,' he said simply, then went on to discuss a project he was initiating at the hospital, while Carrie sat back and listened, her good humour restored.

Their table was secluded, being in an alcove near the leaded light windows. Only the faint hum of voices from the other diners came to her as she listened to Robert Sheraton. She could have gone on listening to his deep, melodic voice all day and far into the night, but all good things came to an end, and, after coffee, they left, Carrie trying to match the surgeon's long stride.

Although it was only February, the sun shone with a surprising amount of warmth now that the rain had cleared. Even the South Downs were free from the light mantle of snow they had worn earlier in the month. Carrie began to feel hot in her numerous jumpers. Judy didn't feel the cold and would probably be wearing a thin jumper, one which showed off her magnificent breasts, and a softly swirling skirt, since she needed to disguise a fair-sized pair of hips.

'Why so sad, little friend?' Mr Sheraton put a comforting arm about her shoulder, and Carrie closed her eyes in bliss for a moment. This was heaven, absolute heaven. If only. . . But she was always thinking that, and it didn't make matters any easier when the surgeon was so close, his breath warming her, the gentle pressure of his arm sending all sorts of erotic thoughts through her mind. To wake up every morning and find him lying there beside her, to watch as he awakened, to be given the right to comfort and protect him, to encourage him, to. . .

'Carrie? You aren't at a loss for words, surely?' Mr Sheraton sounded concerned, anxious, and Carrie didn't know how to reply. She began to shake her head, aware that tears weren't too far away. What could she say? Judy would have known straight away; *she* was never at a loss for words when talking to an eligible man. Damn Judy!

'I—I'm a bit cold, that's all, sir. Thank you,' Carrie said at last.

'Come on, let's get you to the Warriners'. I've a busy afternoon lecturing.' To her delight, Mr Sheraton tucked her arm in his and they strolled companionably to his car.

Then she remembered—Judy would be there and, whatever happened, Mr Sheraton mustn't meet her, he mustn't!

'You don't have to drive me all the way there, really,' she said. 'I like walking, and if you dropped me at the corner of the road before the square—Cavendish Way—that would be fine.'

'Would it? Oh, good.' There was a quiver of laughter in his voice, but to Carrie's relief Mr Sheraton did as she suggested.

'Here we are then, Nurse West—Cavendish Way. Are you sure you can walk the rest of the way on those little legs?'

Since the rest of the way amounted to no more than a few yards, Carrie knew he was being facetious. But it didn't matter, just as long as Judy didn't see him. 'Thank you for the lift, sir. I *can* walk from here,' she said pleasantly, and he chuckled huskily.

'That's a pity, I rather wanted to meet your sister. She sounds interesting.'

Carrie swallowed the sudden lump in her throat. He would, wouldn't he? Hal had been just the same. 'Thank you, but——'

'But no, thanks. Why? Is she so repulsive you have to keep her hidden away, I wonder?' Mr Sheraton said thoughtfully, then tilted Carrie's chin with his forefinger, forcing her to look at him.

For one glorious moment, she thought he was about to kiss her, then she dismissed the idea. That was wishful thinking on a grand scale!

'Remember, Carrie, you have a talent, a very special talent. Don't sit in your sister's shadow. I'll see you.

'Yes, thank you, sir,' she said quickly, then let herself
out of the car, not waiting for him to help her. Then she
ran, not caring what he might think of her. She had to
escape, but from what she was escaping Carrie could not
have said. She only knew that the awful words 'If only,
if only' were drumming inside her head. If this was love,
real love, you could keep it!

'You're later than we expected, Caroline.' That was
Aunt Moira, vaguely disapproving as usual, but Carrie
merely smiled as she kissed her aunt. 'Judy's upstairs.
She says she needs to recover from a heavy morning
shopping. Heaven knows what she's bought,' her aunt
went on peevishly.

'Something for us all, I expect,' Carrie said lightly,
then paused, her eyes puzzled. 'Are you all right, Aunt
Moira? You look. . .' She hesitated, for it was difficult
to say *how* her aunt looked. Certainly not well, that was
for sure.

'I'm fine, thank you. Don't fuss, there's a good girl.'

Dismissed, Carrie made her way slowly up the broad
winding staircase. Aunt Moira hated fuss, but, even so,
Carrie thought she might have a word with Uncle
Charles. Then she flung open the bedroom door, and
beamed at Judy, who eyed her groggily.

'Hello, little one! Still healing the sick, are you? God,
I don't know how you do it.' Judy sat up and swung her
rather long legs over the side of the twin bed.

They hugged each other, and Carrie tried to show how
pleased she was to see Judy again. And, of course, she
was. Though only the six years separated them, Carrie
had rather grown up in awe of Judy, and throughout her
school days had referred every little problem to her,
asking her advice and trying desperately to take it, even
though it hadn't been, she now realised, always sensible
advice.

The positions were somewhat reversed now, and
occasionally Judy would ask for help in solving her
problems, usually of the man-of-the-moment variety.

Carrie now kept her own counsel, made her own mistakes. If only she could ask Judy's advice about the big problem she had in the shape of Mr Robert Sheraton!

Judy made room for her on the bed. This she did by ruthlessly flinging books, felt-pens, writing materials and the like on to the floor. 'There! We can be comfy now. Take your shoes off and relax, little one—you've a couple of days to yourself.'

Carrie beamed. 'Yes! No bedpans, TPR rounds, ward reports. . .' She stopped. 'I wonder how Mrs Hyde is getting on? She's in for——'

Judy shuddered, her generous mouth opening in silent protest. 'No, I won't listen to you!' She covered her ears with her hands. 'I don't want to hear any gory details about operations, thank you very much! What's your consultant like?' she went on, catching Carrie unawares.

Carrie flushed, watched through narrowed blue eyes by her sister. 'Kind,' she muttered. 'You know how gynaes are. No, I suppose you don't, your ward was medical, wasn't it?' she rushed on.

Judy made a moue. 'There's no need to remind me that I survived only *one* ward, Nurse Caroline West! Are you sure he's kind? That wasn't the description Aunt Moira gave me. She's quite keen on him! Wouldn't believe that a romantic heart rested in that iron bosom, would you?'

'Keen? is she? Oh, well, she invited him to Sunday lunch once and——'

'More than once, my child, more than once. She says he's tall, dark and handsome, like some romantic hero. And all you can say is that he's kind! What *has* St Hilda's done to you, pet? You used to be such a romantic soul, always falling in love. Do you remember that tall, rangy sort of boy with green eyes and freckles? I can't remember his name, but——

'Andy Collins,' Carrie said faintly. 'Did he have freckles. Anyway, that was *years* ago! I'd forgotten him,' she said, not entirely truthfully.

'And what about Tom? I can't recall his last name, but he——'

'Tunstall, Tom Tunstall,' Carrie said stolidly, lowering her gaze and picking idly at the quilt. 'I went to his wedding, and they've got a baby now. He married one of the girls in my set, don't you remember?'

'Did he? No, I don't remember a girl, only Tom. He was rather nice, but *so* serious. And there was Hal, wasn't there?' Judy went on brightly, and seemed not to see Carrie flinch.

'Hal? Oh, yes, the registrar. We have so many dishy registrars, I'd definitely forgotten him,' Carrie assured her. Hal was her first real love, the one man she had gone for in a big way. And he had liked her, seemed fond of her. Her gaze softened, her eyes gazing back into the past. Was it only a year ago? She had supposed Judy to have forgotten him, forgotten the young man she had bewitched then pushed aside when someone better came along.

'I haven't. Forgotten Hal, I mean. I wonder where he is now?' Judy continued, then got up and stretched those big, round breasts thrusting against the thin jumper.

Carrie looked up, her expression veiled. No way was she going to let Judy know how much she had cared for Hal. Judy would treat it as a great joke, then she would be sorry, sorry that she had spirited away a man her little sister had loved. Pity or even sympathy was something Carrie couldn't take. Judy couldn't help the way men fell over themselves to get to her; she hadn't *meant* to steal Hal, it just happened, and now Carrie wanted the episode closed. One thing was for sure; she meant to see that Judy din't get a chance to bewitch Robert Sheraton in the same way!

If she thought that the subject of the consultant gynae was closed, she had underestimated Judy. Their aunt's description had obviously intrigued her, and she meant to throw out her lures, just to see what she caught.

Carrie knew the signs but was powerless to do anything about it.

'You must invite this dishy Mr Sheraton to dinner while I'm here, Aunt Moira, dear,' Judy began brightly as they sat drinking tea later that day. 'All Carrie could tell me about him was that he's kind! Would you believe that? So I think you must have been spinning me a line about him being tall and handsome! I don't believe he's anything of the kind.'

Aunt Moira began to protest. 'He is! Really, Judy, I don't suppose Caroline noticed him that much. He's far too senior for you, isn't he?' This remark was addressed in a vague way to Carrie, who ignored it, knowing that no answer was expected. 'He made the poor girl so nervous that she dropped one of my saucers—one of my *best* saucers,' she went on. 'Consultants don't notice learners, of course, not in *that* way. Anyway, he's very tied up. I've asked him twice since then and he's always busy. Of course, they entertain a great deal, I believe. Charles and I have been to dinner there once, at his aunt's, that is, and you wouldn't believe the luxury! A butler, no less! The only butlers I've seen have been on the television,' Aunt Moira went on, clearly impressed, while Carrie opened her mouth in dismay.

Mr Sheraton had a butler! He *was* rich, then. Ella had said that, Carrie recalled now, but she hadn't paid that much attention. Then she remembered the housekeeper. 'Ella told me they had a housekeeper!' she protested. 'She didn't mention a butler.'

Judy turned to her, wide-eyed, and Carrie cursed her runaway tongue. '*Who*, might I ask, is Ella?' When Carrie hesitated, Judy playfully boxed her ears. 'Come on now, junior, tell all!'

'That's what he calls Mireille, my dear,' Aunt Moira put in. 'She's his daughter. She's about thirteen, I think, rather a spoilt child. But of course he's devoted to her.'

'*Is* he? Well, well.' Judy sat back, her appraising gaze upon Carrie. 'Why didn't you tell me about her, little

one? And *how* do you come to know the consultant's
daughter?'

Carrie hesitantly explained about Ella's operation.
'She's due for discharge now. She's probably gone and I
don't expect to see her again,' Carrie hurried on. 'She's
rather a pet.'

'And is *he* rather a pet, too ? Or aren't you saying?'
Judy teased, causing Carrie to colour.

'For heaven's sake, Judy, don't tease the girl! You
know how she sulks,' Aunt Moira said sharply, and
before Carrie could prepare her defence at such an
unkind remark their aunt went on to discuss the spring
bazaar. As far as Carrie knew, the question of the
consultant and his daughter passed from her sister's
mind. Since Judy led such an interesting life, this was
hardly surprising. A book-signing tour sounded exciting
and Carrie rather envied her.

'Where will you go? All around the country or just
Sussex?' Carrie asked later as they prepared for bed.
They were to share the rather cramped guest-room, since
Aunt Moira didn't intend putting herself out, even for
her favourite niece. She didn't, Carrie conceded, look all
that well and having the two of them to stay must be an
added burden for such a busy woman.

In the bedroom, there was just enough space for the
twin beds plus an ancient chest of drawers and a
wardrobe. Judy had brought masses of clothes with her
and it was difficult to believe she was there only for a
week. Carrie's clothing consisted of a dress plus a clean
blouse and underwear and an extra jumper, and these
were soon tucked away.

'The book-signing? Oh, yes, we're going to, let me
see——' Judy thumbed through the pages of the huge
diary. 'We're kicking off at Brighton, then it's—— Do
you fancy him?'

Startled, Carrie glanced up, her nightgown clutched
defensively to her chest. But before she could hotly deny
such a thing Judy nodded slowly.

'Yes, I can see you do. He's too old for you, surely? All consultants are at least forty, aren't they? They always *seem* at least forty, anyway. All that responsibility sobers them up!'

'He isn't forty and no, I don't fancy him—if you mean Mr Sheraton,' Carrie rushed on. 'He's very good, but a bit autocratic. I don't think he notices learners and even if he *did* I wouldn't be interested! Really.'

'Aha! The lady protests too much,' Judy said lightly, stretching out on top of the bed, her shapely body inadequately covered by what looked like a scrap of sea-green gauze. 'I really must investigate him, little one. Yes, I really must.' Smiling to herself, Judy turned onto her side and eyed Carrie shrewdly. 'Even if you do fancy him, there's no shame in that, surely? I expect most of the young nurses do.'

Carrie nodded. 'Well, yes, quite a few of them; not Ann, though. You remember Ann Haynes, don't you? She came up to London with me last year?' At Judy's nod, Carrie went on to talk about Ann, neatly turning the conversation away from the consultant.

As she lay sleepless, Carrie wondered whether Judy would take the matter any further. Knowing her, she probably would. It wasn't fair, it wasn't! Carrie sat up and hugged her knees to her small breasts, before glancing at the other bed, only a foot or so away from her own. Judy's breathing was regular; *she* wasn't lying awake dreaming of a certain man. Tears sprang to Carrie's eyes and she bit her lip savagely. If Judy chose to inspect Robert Sheraton, there was no hope for anyone else, not even Sister Whitworth and certainly not Sister Carter. And not little Student Nurse West, either.

She lay back, thinking dark thoughts, then sat up again. No! She wouldn't give in this time! She would fight for Robert Sheraton, no matter how mesmerising he found Judy. Yes, this time she would fight back. Hal hadn't been worth fighting for, but this man was.

That she had no right to fight for, or over, him, Carrie had to concede, but she certainly wasn't going to let Judy take him away. Even if she was saving him for Sister Whitworth, Carrie meant to save him!

CHAPTER EIGHT

LIFE on Marigold Ward seemed rather flat after Carrie's time off, and she suspected that she secretly envied her sister's racier lifestyle. Judy never meant to do so, but she always made Carrie feel that she had missed out on life, that nursing was one of the dullest professions imaginable and that all there was to look forward to was promotion to ward sister and possibly marriage to a dull doctor in due course!

Of course nursing wasn't like that. At times it *was* exciting, though drudgery and hard work played a large part, but it was never dull or boring. People couldn't be boring and she dealt with people every day. No, Judy was wrong, Carrie mused as she tested a sample of urine the morning of her return. Nursing wasn't dull, but. . .

But since Mr Sheraton was away for a few days at some meeting or other Marigold Ward certainly *was* dull! Carrie turned sharply at a sound from the doorway, half hoping. . .But it was Ann, and Carrie wondered what sort of mood her friend would be in. With Ann, one never knew. Sometimes it was like walking on eggshells—one tiny false step and everything cracked.

'Hello, there!' Ann greeted her breezily enough. 'Had a good time with Uncle Charles Warriner?'

'Brill,' Carrie said shortly, her mind on her task once more. 'No, nothing wrong with that, a nice specimen,' she murmured. 'Is Sister still off the ward? I wanted to ask about my project.'

'What? No, she's just come back. And Carrie, guess what? She knows someone who'll let us have a house! Imagine, a whole house to rent!'

'That's lovely!' Carrie was pleased for her friend. She

knew Phil hadn't been keen on the flat they had been offered. 'Who owns it?'

'That's the strangest thing. It belongs to someone in the hospital, Sister thinks, but she doesn't know who. And Mrs Jordan—you remember Mrs Jordan—well, *she's* been found somewhere, as well, though hers is only temporary.'

'Great! I'll bet she's pleased. Did you see her off?' Eileen Jordan had been discharged while Carrie was off and she had hoped to kiss the woman goodbye, tell her not to worry too much, but she had missed out on that, too, as well as on seeing Ella Sheraton off. 'And what about Ella? No, I suppose you wouldn't see her.'

'Ella? Oh, you mean Mr Sheraton's daughter! Yes, she popped in to see Sister and thank her. *Daddy* brought her, all casually dressed and handsomer than ever,' Ann went on, with a little laugh.

'Oh? Was Sister Whitworth with them?' Carrie asked, pretending unconcern as she washed her hands.

'Sister Whitworth? No, should she have been? Oh, yes, they're having a big romance, aren't they? I still don't think she's his type, but consultants are odd birds.' Ann tripped away before Carrie could find something cutting to say.

Carrie found Sister Carter in a happy mood, almost pleasant for once, and the thought crossed her mind that perhaps Mr Sheraton had invited her to stay at his house. Surely he didn't really have a butler?

'Ah, Nurse West. Had a nice time off? Good, good. Now,' Sister went on without waiting for any remark Carrie might wish to make, 'close the door, there's a good girl. Don't want everyone knowing about our good fortune, do we?'

Surprised, Carrie did as she was told, then stood in front of her senior, wondering what sort of good fortune they were to share. 'Is the ward to be upgraded, Sister? Is that our good fortune?'

'Upgraded? Oh, you mean the new hangings we

wanted. Our Mr Sheraton's been on to the committee, though it's really the sort of thing the Friends of St Hilda's provide. Never mind that. Look.' She thrust the duty roster in front of Carrie's eyes. 'I've arranged for you to have the whole weekend off, but you will have to get someone to work those last two hours on the Friday for you. I can't do any more re-arranging.'

'But I don't want the weekend off!' Carrie cried. 'It means I'll have to stay with——' She broke off, and shuffled uncomfortably. 'Please, I'd rather work at the weekend. Ann Haynes might like it off.'

'I dare say she would but she isn't being honoured, *you* are.' Sister frowned suddenly. 'Didn't Mr Sheraton mention it to you?'

'Mention what, Sister?'

'No, I can see he didn't. That's very right and proper; it might not have suited me to let you have the time off. Well, there's an invitation for both of us to join young Ella Sheraton at the weekend. You're to go along to keep her company, Mr Sheraton says,' Sister announced, as calmly as if she had been discussing the ward schedule.

A weekend with Robert Sheraton! Varied expressions chased themselves across Carrie's small face. A whole weekend! Of course, Sister would be there. . . 'Is that the house with the butler, please, Sister?' was all she could think to say, but it was the right thing, for Sister Carter had been eyeing her suspiciously.

Now she laughed. 'That's just the sort of remark I would expect from you, Nurse West!'

'Yes, Sister,' Carrie said politely, relieved that her senior's suspicious look had gone.

'It isn't Mr Sheraton who has a butler, it's his aunt. She's an Honourable something or other. It's her home we'll be visiting. She might have a footman, as well. I wonder?'

Since Sister seemed to be interested in the question of servants, Carrie obligingly fed her with suitable questions, and the next ten minutes passed very pleasantly

for them both. They were recalled to their work when a
brisk tap at the door announced the arrival of their house
doctor, and Carrie was shooed away. She went back to
her mundane tasks, in a whirl of rainbow-coloured
dreams. She was to spend the weekend with Robert
Sheraton, in what sounded like a stately home! Just let
Judy try to tell her that hospitals were dull places!

There had been two new admissions while Carrie was
on her days off, and one of these ladies began signalling
urgently to her. Carrie moved towards her with her usual
cheery smile, but now it was even more cheery.

'Look like you've been left a fortune, dearie!' the new
patient remarked. 'Get us a bedpan, there's a duck.'

'Yes, right away, Mrs Murray.' Whistling a little tune
under her breath, Carrie sped away on her errand, and
was still beaming when she returned with the bedpan.
'Here we are, then.' Briskly she whisked the curtains
around the bed and placed the warmed bedpan in
position. 'Is that comfy?'

'Lovely. You've warmed it, too. You're a good girl.
One of the other nurses said as how they missed you
when you wasn't on the ward. "Our Carrie's got a lovely
beaming smile", she said, and you have, love.' Mrs
Murray settled down to use the bedpan, and a delighted
Carrie left her in peace, wondering who had said such a
nice thing about her.

Remarks like that made it all worthwhile, the drudgery, the long, unsocial hours, the poor pay, the harsh
words from seniors who thought students were slaves,
the sad time when no more could be done for a favourite
patient. Yes, Judy didn't know what she had missed.

'Daydreaming, Nurse West?' a familiar voice asked,
and Carrie spun round. Surely he was away?

'The meeting was cancelled, Nurse, so it *is* me,' the
deep brown voice went on calmly, and she nodded, her
fingers twisting the rubber apron she wore.

'Yes, sir.' Her voice was inaudible. Then she remembered the treat she had been promised, and she met the

surgeon's gaze. 'Thank you, sir! For the weekend, I mean,' she said quietly. 'Is Ella all right now?'

'Yes, and keen to see you again. I'm too old and dull to be of any use, it seems.' Robert Sheraton frowned, and Carrie very nearly put out a hand towards him, meaning to offer comfort. Just in time, she remembered.

'I'll try to keep her occupied, sir. While you entertain Sister Carter,' she said primly, and dark grey eyes glinted with an emotion Carrie couldn't be certain of.

'Ah, yes, Sister Carter. Yes, I'm looking forward to the weekend,' he said solemnly. 'Now, while I'm here I'll see Mrs Murray.' He glanced down the ward towards the bed curtains.

'No! She's on the bedpan, sir. Shall I come and tell you when she's finished?'

'Yes, do that, Nurse West, do that,' he murmured, before going into the office, leaving Carrie as pleased as if she *had* been left a fortune.

Much as Sister Carter had looked forward to her weekend with the consultant, it wasn't to be, and it was Carrie alone who set out on what she just knew would be the best weekend she had ever spent.

Of course she felt sorry for Sister, coming down with that awful tummy bug just then, and had offered to work during the weekend to help cover the ward. But Marigold Ward could manage, so the weekend was hers and hers alone!

Carrie's eyes gleamed as she waited in the lobby of St Hilda's for Mr Sheraton's familiar car to pick her up on the Friday evening. She huddled into her anorak, for the evening was chilly, and there was the faintest hint of sleet in the air, with the weather forecasters promising more to come.

A car stopped in front of her and flashed its headlights, and eagerly Carrie stepped forward. Then she remembered that she ought not to look *too* eager, and hastily composed her face into what she hoped was its normal expression. Mr Sheraton, snug in his sheepskin coat, got out, but it was the woman who sat beside him who caught Carrie's attention. It was Aunt Moira!

'Try to look as if you're pleased to see me, Caroline!' Her aunt's voice was as sharp as usual, and she looked far from pleased to be there. 'Do get in, there's a good girl.'

Mr Sheraton came around to open the rear door for Carrie, whose mind had gone numb. She still had the remains of the smile upon her face, and indeed she felt that her face had become fixed in that caricature of a smile. Aunt Moira! What on earth was she doing here?

'Since Sister Carter couldn't come this time, Nurse, I invited Mrs Warriner. Can't have you coming unchaperoned, can we?' he murmured, these last words spoken so softly that only Carrie could hear them.

She nodded, understanding. He was fearful for his reputation, which was only to be expected. But she hardly thought having a student nurse at his home for the weekend would occasion comment. After all, they wouldn't be alone—there would be Ella, and probably his aunt. And the butler and half a dozen footmen, she thought, a little giggle escaping her. Yes, the weekend promised to be an interesting and unusual one, even if Moira Warriner was there to make cutting remarks and to pour cold water on any little scheme she might get up to amuse Ella.

'We aren't going to my own home, Nurse,' Mr Sheraton explained formally as he set the car in motion and turned carefully out of the St Hilda's entrance. 'Ella's staying with my aunt Aggie until she's better. It's a bit dull for her and she'll be glad of your company.'

'I'll be glad to see her again, sir. Thank you for asking me,' Carrie said, equally formally, aware that her aunt was eyeing her.

'Ella hoped to come along with me, but I thought it too cold for her. Anyway, she's got company,' the consultant added, and Carrie pricked up her ears.

'Has she got a friend staying, then?'

'It's Miss Nugent, Caroline, and please don't be inquisitive,' Aunt Moira hissed, turning round to glare at Carrie.

'Oh,' said Carrie, wondering who on earth Miss Nugent was, and rather afraid she was yet another friend of Robert Sheraton's!

The drive was a long one, and Carrie peered out of the window, trying to see where they were. Then a lighted road sign caught her eye. They were on the Brighton road, but just as she was about to remark on it the surgeon turned off on to a narrower, only dimly lit road and she was completely lost.

'That was Firle Place, over on your left. Too late, I'm afraid,' Mr Sheraton called. 'Have you been there?'

'No, I haven't. I've never been to a stately home,' Carrie confessed. 'Oh, yes, I have! When I was at school we went on a trip to Knole.'

There was a smile in his voice. 'I'm afraid my aunt Aggie's place is hardly Knole, but I think you'll like it, Carrie.'

Her first name had slipped out unconsciously, Carrie knew, and from her aunt's sharp intake of breath she had noticed it, and would draw her own conclusions.

They moved on into the night and Carrie tried to sit back, but was too excited, too overwrought. She wondered what Aunt Aggie would be like, and, most of all, she wondered about Miss Nugent. They saw the lights of Merehurst soon after they passed through the tall, wrought-iron entrance gates, which stood open in silent welcome.

'This is it, ladies! Welcome to Merehurst!' the surgeon said, and Aunt Moira leaned forward, obviously impressed, as they were driven along a wide drive which curved slightly to the left before straightening out again. Carrie's heart began to flutter painfully. Mr Sheraton had a very rich relative if she could afford to live here. She sighed, and his quick ears picked up the sound.

'Tired, Nurse? I expect you are. Ops day is always busy for you nurses.' There was sympathy in his voice, almost as though he knew how hard surgical nurses worked on ops days, and Carrie was quick to assure him that she wasn't a bit tired.

Mr Sheraton turned into the carriage sweep in front of imposing double doors, which stood open. 'I believe Ella's come to meet you.'

It was indeed Ella, and Carrie was scarcely out of the car before the girl came running over. 'Oh, Carrie, you came! Daddy said you might not and it's *ever* so boring!'

After greeting Aunt Moira politely, Ella tugged at Carrie's hand. 'Come inside and see my den! It's got everything! Oh, don't worry about the luggage,' Ella went on, as Carrie glanced back. 'Bert will see to it—he's been here years and years. Come and meet Sarah and Aunt Aggie. Then you can come and see your room. It's right next to mine.'

Carrie was disappointed not to see a butler, but found herself almost propelled into a spacious, high-ceilinged room which might have come from the pages of *Country Life*. She caught a glimpse of a huge marble fireplace, where a log fire crackled in a welcoming way, and found her feet sinking into a deep pile carpet as she made her way towards the occupants of the room.

A tall, elderly lady who could only be Great-Aunt Aggie rose as Carrie approached, and put her glass down on the antique table at her side, but it was her companion who caught Carrie's eyes. She was in a wheelchair!

'This is Nurse Carrie West, Aunt Aggie,' Ella said formally, and Carrie took the hand extended to her. Aunt Aggie's grip was firm and strong, despite her advanced years, and slate-grey eyes twinkled at her, eyes so like the surgeon's yet friendlier, lacking that certain chilliness that often appeared in Mr Sheraton's.

'My great-aunt, Mrs Weston,' Ella said. 'And this is Sarah—Miss Sarah Nugent, a friend of Daddy's.' Ella indicated the woman in the wheelchair, and Carrie went across to shake her hand.

Miss Nugent was in her late twenties or early thirties, Carrie judged, and had the sweetest smile she had seen for a long time. 'I've heard so much about you from Ella that I feel I know you, Nurse West.' Her voice was low and clear and definitely upper crust, and Carrie felt tongue-tied and awkward, the way she often felt when in the company of her sister and father.

'I hope Ella hasn't been boring you with tales about Nurse West,' Carrie managed, shakily. 'I didn't really see a lot of her, because she was in the private wing and I. . .' Her voice trailed off, as Miss Nugent's gaze moved from her, the pale blue eyes brightening.

'Come in, Robert! You've been ages!'

'Sorry—I popped into one of my wards first.' Mr Sheraton's smile was warm, and, judging by the way Sarah Nugent's face lit up, there was definitely a romance there. Well, hard luck Sister Carter, Sister Whitworth and Nurse West!

A saddened Carrie trailed up the grand staircase behind Ella. No, there was no place for her in Robert Sheraton's life. How could she ever have thought there was? She saw now that her dreams were the dreams of a naïve little nurse who thought that all he needed was lots of TLC. She didn't belong in his world. She emitted a little sigh, and Ella's sharp ears picked it up.

'You aren't sorry you've come, are you? I wanted you. It's *so* dull here, you wouldn't believe it,' Ella said, her gaze anxious as it rested upon Carrie's flushed face.

'Of course I'm not sorry! I'm rather tired, to tell you the truth. We nearly had Sister Carter, too—did you know?'

'Daddy told me. I can't think why he asked her, but he said you ought to have a chaperon. But there's Sarah—she would have done. Do you like her? I do, lots,' Ella prattled on, stopping only when she led the way into a room which looked far too large to be a mere bedroom.

'Is this your room?' Carrie asked, bemused.

'No, silly! It's yours. Well, for the weekend, anyway. I'll get them to keep it for you—you'll come again, won't you?' Ella begged. 'You might come every weekend.'

Carrie smiled at her enthusiasm. 'I can't come *every* weekend, Ella. Most weekends I have to work. I prefer to work, really,' she confessed, surveying her surroundings. The furniture was modern, rather to her surprise. A divan bed was covered with a beautiful silver lace bedspread, and there was a small chest of drawers, an oval dressing-table, and a double wardrobe. In one corner there was a comfortable-looking brocade-covered easy chair and a couple of other chairs, plus a writing desk over by the window, where rich pink velvet curtains were drawn against the night.

'There's a lovely view over the parkland. As soon as it's light, you'll see,' Ella promised, clapping her hands together, a gesture which reminded Carrie that the girl was only thirteen. Yet how sophisticated and grown-up she seemed now, set against her own surroundings. The velvet bolero suit she wore made her look about sixteen, and she was wearing her hair up. The grey eyes and sooty lashes belonged to her father, but the creamy complexion and air of elegance came from her mother, Carrie thought, feeling rather gauche and clumsy.

Then, irritably, she shrugged the thought aside. Too many years of living in Judy's shadow had taken their toll. Here she was, wallowing in what might be called self-pity, and she hadn't asked Ella how she was.

'I was going to ask you how you are, but I can see— you're looking fitter than I am,' Carrie commented, and Ella laughed.

'That's what Sarah says. She says she wishes she could run about like me. Do you like her?' Ella rushed on, without giving Carrie time to consider. 'She's fun, not a bit stuffy or—or self-pitying, I suppose.'

'She's got a lovely smile,' Carrie acknowledged wistfully. 'Has she always been disabled? I shouldn't ask, but being a nurse I——'

'That's all right, Sarah won't mind. Yes, she's been in a wheelchair ever since I can remember. She had a riding accident years ago. She's always been around,' the girl went on thoughtfully. 'Daddy loves her,' she said, peering at Carrie from under those dark lashes, and Carrie composed her face into what she hoped was merely polite interest. So, she had been right about Miss Nugent!

CHAPTER NINE

ROBERT SHERATON glanced up just as Carrie paused in the doorway of the drawing-room a little later, and his smile seemed to be for her alone. 'Come along in, Nurse West. Sherry?' He paused by the cocktail cabinet, the bottle raised, but Carrie shook her head.

'No, thank you. Could I have a soft drink, please?' she asked. Her throat was dry and a bitter lemon was what she really needed, though she didn't think that would ease the dryness. Tension, she told herself, anxiety, fear of the unknown. Just recently, they had started lectures on the psychological aspects of illness and she recognised the symptoms—she was suffering from the beginnings of a stately-home phobia!

'Of course.' He bent over the drinks. 'There's lemonade if you would like? Ella will have a lemonade, I expect. Or there's squash, bitter lemon——'

'Bitter lemon would be fine. Thank you, sir,' Carrie said politely, and her host shot her an amused look. Only Carrie correctly interpreted it as meaning, 'You're very polite all of a sudden, Student Nurse West!'

She bit her lip in an effort to stop the laughter which was bubbling away inside but wasn't successful. To her surprise, Mr Sheraton joined in, his pleasant chuckle warming her, chasing away the phobia. There was nothing to fear, after all.

Out of the corner of her eye, Carrie saw Miss Nugent glance at them, first at Robert then at her, then back to him again. 'Is it a private joke, Robert, dear, or may we all share it?' she asked, pleasantly enough, but Carrie was relieved when the consultant shook his head.

Brushing back the lock of hair which kept falling over one eye, he merely smiled. 'It's a private St Hilda's joke—isn't it, Nurse West? We can't share it with lay people.'

'That's right, sir. Hospital secret,' Carrie said brightly, then went forward to accept the glass of bitter lemon from him. Their hands touched briefly and Carrie silently cursed herself for the way her hand trembled. Surely he must notice? Apparently he did not, for he smiled across at his daughter.

'Lemonade, puss?'

'Yes, please, Daddy. I told Carrie she could come every weekend. Can't she have weekends off? I'm sure she could if she asked,' the girl went on confidently, and Carrie hid a wry smile. Persistence wasn't in it!

'If that was a broad hint for me to use my limited influence, then, no, it can't be done, Ella. I'm sorry, but Nurse West has to work weekends. It's part of the minus side of being a nurse,' he explained gently.

'Oh!' Ella sipped her lemonade, her gaze pensive, and Carrie wondered what new scheme she was hatching. Evidently she wasn't used to being thwarted. Really, the girl needed a mother, Carrie thought yet again, and no sooner the thought than her gaze shifted towards Sarah Nugent.

It came as a shock to find that Miss Nugent was looking at *her*, and Carrie wondered uneasily whether she had given herself away. If the woman were to suggest to Aunt Moira that there was something between nurse and surgeon, all hell would be let loose, and that wasn't an exaggeration!

Carrie shrugged away the unpalatable thought, then crossed over to Sarah Nugent. 'I saw you looking at me. Is there anything I can do for you?' she asked with her usual warm smile.

'In a nursing capacity, you mean?' Miss Nugent's smile was wry. 'No, there's nothing that can be done. Robert would have seen to it, you may be sure. I've been like this since a riding accident when I wasn't much older than Ella. It's permanent, I'm afraid, but you mustn't think I wallow in self-pity, Nurse,' she went on quickly.

'Oh, no, I'm sure you don't,' Carrie said. 'Do you have any contact with the disabled association? I hardly remember my mother, but I know she was in a wheel-chair—that's why I'm interested.'

'Yes, I help out the Gainsborough Association for the Disabled. Even in a wheelchair, there are things I can do to help them. I can type, for instance, and I act as a sort of social secretary for the organisation, arranging half-day drives, holidays, that sort of thing,' Miss Nugent told her. 'What was the matter with your mother? Do you remember?'

'She had MS—multiple sclerosis,' Carrie said slowly. She could remember only a frail, shadowy figure, some-one for whom the disease had taken a rapid course. Her early memories of Aunt Moira were stronger, more real to her. 'I used to do little things for my mother, but I scarcely knew her. I don't remember her when she was well, anyway,' she confessed.

'Yes, it's a terrible affliction in its later stages,' Miss Nugent agreed, 'though I have a friend with it and she stays pretty well most of the time. She certainly isn't in a wheelchair, and many people with it can live a long and reasonably active life and never get wheelchair-bound. Now, tell me about St Hilda's,' she invited, and Carrie was glad to change the subject.

Once or twice, she felt Robert Sheraton's eyes upon them as they sat side by side, Miss Nugent in her specially padded chair, Carrie on a high-seat chair in the corner by the fire. He didn't come over to them, though, rather to Carrie's relief. Being too near the surgeon was bad for her nerves, and she had the feeling that Sarah Nugent's shrewd gaze saw far too much.

A welcome respite came when the short but, in Carrie's eyes, imposing butler put in an appearance, announcing that a light supper was ready in the morning-room, and Mrs Weston, leaning on Robert Sheraton's arm, led her guests along the richly panelled hall towards a door at the rear of the house.

If Carrie had expected footmen to bow them into the room, she was to be disappointed. Miss Nugent told her that Simons, the butler, was the only full-time staff, the rest of the household consisting of a cook-housekeeper who came in daily, and various part-time cleaners. 'I suppose I'm the nearest Aunt Aggie has to a companion,' Miss Nugent added. 'I think even Buckingham Palace has difficulty in getting live-in servants these days!'

Since Miss Nugent's wheelchair wasn't powered, it naturally fell to Carrie's lot to push it and she was glad of something positive to do. Robert Sheraton brought up the rear and Ella walked beside the chair, carrying on a cheerful conversation. Carrie herself was silent. It hurt, being near to him and unable to do more than smile politely. Having to keep her silly love for him hidden away was imposing a strain upon her. Having to keep it hidden from everyone in the household was an even greater strain, and her eyes involuntarily sought those of Miss Nugent, who was glancing towards the surgeon.

Miss Nugent's smile was turned upon her now, and Carrie sensed the understanding behind that smile. She knew! Oh, how awful! Waves of colour shot up Carrie's face and she stumbled as they turned through the wide doorway.

'Careful!' Robert Sheraton's hand shot out to steady her, but Carrie pulled away.

'It's all right, sir, really,' she mumbled. 'I'm sorry, Miss Nugent.' She smiled down at the woman. 'Did I give you a shock? Will you stay in your chair, or shall I——'

'You're not on duty now, Nurse West. Let Miss Nugent sort herself out; she isn't helpless. You come and sit beside Ella,' the surgeon instructed, and Carrie turned on him indignantly, her face still flushed.

'Being a nurse doesn't stop at the ward door, Mr Sheraton! With respect,' she went on, then remembered another time when she had said the very same thing. 'I'm glad to be able to help Miss Nugent.'

Robert Sheraton held up his hands in mock surrender. 'All right, I capitulate! Do your Nurse Goodbody act. *I* shall sit next to my daughter instead, and you can sit with your new patient.'

Miss Nugent laughed. 'Take no notice of him, Carrie; he's in one of his autocratic consultant moods! I may call you Carrie, mayn't I? You sit with me, and no, I don't usually stay in my chair but as it's so late I might just as well. We kept supper back for you and your aunt.'

At mention of her aunt, Carrie glanced about. She saw now that Aunt Moira was sitting beside Aunt Aggie, over by the long curtains which shut out the night air. The breakfast-room was small and somehow homely, and Carrie felt more at ease here than she had in the elegant but daunting drawing-room. Ella had told her they didn't use the formal dining-room except when her great aunt was entertaining some 'fussy old body', as she had put it. This was a family room in every sense of the word, and Carrie thought it rather a shame that Ella was the only child to enjoy it. It must be lonely for her.

She must have looked sad, for Sarah Nugent put out a hand to offer her comfort. 'Sad, Carrie? Do you miss your hospital friends?'

'Oh, no! No, not at all. Half of my set are on nights at the moment, so I've got used to being on my own,' Carrie assured her. 'Do you live here all the time?' she went on, anxious to change the subject. 'I mean, is this your home, with Mrs Weston?'

'Just call her Aunt Aggie, she'll love you for it. No, I'm just staying with her. My father's a widower and we live about four miles away. I'm not really needed there, and I tend to spend a lot of time with Aunt Aggie. And Robert, naturally,' she went on, her sharp eyes on Carrie.

'Yes, of course, but Mr Sheraton and Ella don't live here, do they? I thought he had a flat somewhere. Sister Carter mentioned it once,' Carrie rushed on.

'He lives near St Hilda's, but it isn't a flat, it's a smallish house; one of those mock-Georgian houses near Cross Street. Do you know where I mean?'

Carrie nodded. 'They're lovely! Well, I've never been in one,' she had to confess, 'but I like the look of them. Sometimes I pick out the sort of home I'd like one day, and Cross Street is high on my list! If I couldn't live there, I'd like to——'

'Carrie, dear.' Sarah Nugent's voice was low, pitched so that only Carrie herself could hear. 'Carrie, you haven't——' She hesitated, glancing down at her hands, long, slim hands which lay in her lap, and Carrie shifted uneasily, knowing only too well what was coming. 'You aren't in. . . Sometimes, when we're young, we let our imagination run away with us and I wouldn't want you to get hurt. You're too sweet for that,' Miss Nugent went on, obviously picking her words carefully. 'Robert and I have known each other for a long time,' she emphasised. 'I wouldn't want you to mistake his kindness for anything more than it is. I know he's handsome and charismatic, and ——'

'He's a consultant, Miss Nugent,' Carrie said firmly, hoping the woman couldn't hear the painful beating of her heart or the fluttering as her hopes died. 'Consultants and learners have little contact with one another. Most consultants don't even realise that students exist, though, to be fair, Mr Sheraton does. I thought he was awfully autocratic and, well, arrogant, at first,' she hurried on, 'but he isn't really. The patients love him!'

'And do you love him, my dear?' Large blue eyes were turned upon her, and Carrie didn't know what to say.

She decided she wouldn't lie to the woman. Her secret would be safe with Miss Nugent. 'I suppose I do, in a way, but I understand, about not mistaking his kindness, I mean. He *is* just being kind, and he's invited me here only because of Ella. I expect we can explore tomorrow or go for a walk, if it's fine. That's what I'm here for.'

Her voice faltered, despite her resolve, and Miss Nugent let out her pent-up breath.

'I was afraid you would fall for his charms. Haven't you a young man of your own? You're a pretty girl—there must be dozens of young men at the hospital, surely?'

Were there? Carrie hadn't noticed any since Robert Sheraton had entered her life, but she decided to tell Miss Nugent about Phil Mackie. And Hal. Why not? At least it would prove that she wasn't hanging out for a consultant, as her aunt would have termed it.

'I used to have a boyfriend, a doctor at the hospital,' she began cautiously, then all eyes were turned upon her aunt, who moaned softly then clutched at her chest.

Carrie got to her before the surgeon did, and Aunt Moira tried to smile, but didn't quite manage it. 'I'm all right, Caroline,' she murmured. 'It's just this pain. I keep getting it and it won't go away. When I sit down it stops but this time I——'

Robert Sheraton moved Carrie gently to one side, bending his head to whisper in her ear, 'Ambulance, Carrie.'

Carrie sped away to the telephone, leaving her aunt in his care. This was the first time her aunt had mentioned a chest pain, but it all fitted into place. Hadn't Aunt Moira complained of tiredness, or 'utter weariness' as she had put it? Now it seemed that the angina had given place to something more serious—Aunt Moira was a heart-attack victim and she might die.

As if in a dream, Carrie accompanied her aunt in the ambulance, though there was nothing she could do other than hold the limp, sweaty hand and pray. Of course, people recovered; it wasn't always fatal, she knew that. Yet it hurt her to think of Aunt Moira suffering, perhaps for weeks, and no one, not even her husband, being aware of the true nature of her suffering. Aunt Moira was always grumbling about something and after a while one simply shut one's ears to her grumbles, a case of crying wolf once too often.

ITU was cold and impersonal, Carrie felt, but the sister's smile was warm and welcoming and helped chip away some of the ice which had settled around Carrie's heart. 'Don't you worry about your aunt, Nurse. We're experts here,' the sister assured her, putting a comforting arm about her shoulders. 'Is she your favourite aunt?'

'She's my only aunt. She—she helped bring me up after my mother died,' Carrie explained, realising belatedly how much she owed Aunt Moira. Tears welled up but she blinked them away. Tears solved nothing and it was unforgivable for a nurse to cry when there was work to be done. 'Is there anything I can do for Aunt Moira?'

The sister shook her head. 'No, not really. Leave it all to us. You can stay if you wish but I think you would do better going home. We'll be in touch—Dr Warriner will be here soon, so don't worry.'

Home. Where was home? Back to the nurses' home, Carrie supposed. Yes, that would be best. At least she would be on the spot if anything happened. But she would wait for Uncle Charles first.

'Hello, my dear,' He managed a wan smile when they met at the hatchway of ITU, then he squeezed her hand. 'Off you go, Carrie, back to your room, I think. I'll let you know the moment there's any news and there's nothing you can do here.'

Carrie shook her head. 'Don't be silly, I couldn't leave you. I'll just pop back to my room and change, then I'll come back here. *Someone* has to look after you!' she finished lightly. 'After all, I'm that cheery Nurse West!'

She was rewarded by the glimmer of a smile. 'Good girl, I'll see you later. Oh, by the way, Judy was wondering what she could do, but I told her there wasn't anything. Nothing *I* can do, come to that. Give her a ring, there's a good girl—set her mind at rest.'

Carrie doubted that Judy's mind was still on her aunt,

but agreed with her uncle's request. It would be something to do, anything to relieve the tension.

How quiet the hospital was at night. It reminded Carrie of her spell of night duty before Christmas. Reminded her, too, of her first meeting with the arrogant Robert Sheraton. It seemed years ago, and she felt she had aged at least ten years in that time. Or had she simply grown up?

She pondered on that as she hurried along the silent corridors—silent, that was, save for the occasional swish of a ward door, or distant sounds from the canteen or the kitchens. Here and there, too, she heard the faint murmur of voices, but mostly there was just the silence of a great building slumbering, and she felt quite alone. The tears that she had angrily checked earlier now came, and she cried softly, for her aunt, for herself, and for Robert Sheraton and their still-born love.

Her room boasted a small washbasin and she decided she would wash her face and tidy herself before going back to sit with her uncle. A change of clothing wouldn't come amiss, either, she mused, glancing down at the black skirt and pretty lilac jumper she wore—clothes she had chosen to impress Robert Sheraton. What a fool she was!

She stood in silence for a long moment, her mind in turmoil. If only. . . Then, aware that she was time-wasting, she washed and changed, and was about to brush her hair when there was a quick tap at her door. Thinking it was one of her friends, she called out, but the door didn't open.

'It's all right, come in!' With a sigh, Carrie opened the door—to find Robert Sheraton in the doorway, his face grave. She didn't need to ask, she could read the answer to her unspoken question in his eyes.

'Carrie, my dear, I'm so very sorry,' he whispered against her hair, as, somehow, she found herself in his arms. He came into the room, kicking the door shut.

'I ought to have hurried but I——' Carrie broke off.

She knew she must hurry, yet she had wasted time in changing, then in daydreaming about what it would be like in Robert Sheraton's arms. Now she *was* in his arms, but her moment of triumph had turned to ashes.

Then, very gently, his lips touched her hair, and with a small sigh, Carrie snuggled closer, her body moulding itself against his. Those same lips trailed down her cheeks, then found her mouth, softly, hesitantly.

The kiss was the sweetest she had ever known, as Robert's questing mouth found hers again and again. Then his lips moved to her eyelids and kissed them, too. 'My poor Carrie, my poor little darling,' he murmured, and Carrie closed her eyes tightly, against the world. There were just the two of them, herself and Robert Sheraton, and no one else mattered, not Sister Whitworth, not Miss Nugent. If only it could always be like this. . .

CHAPTER TEN

IT SEEMED so right, being held against Robert's muscular chest, that Carrie made a small murmur of protest when at length he put her away from him, his breathing harsh. Then, as if drawn by some invisible thread, they moved together again, their lips meeting in a kiss of searing passion. Carrie's legs trembled, and she could feel her heart racing away. She knew if Robert made some move towards her bed, that virginal single bed, she could not have resisted him, didn't *want* to resist him. This was so right!

But he didn't. Abruptly he dropped his arms and turned away from her for a long moment, then moved towards the door.

Fearing that he was leaving her, Carrie put out her hand. 'No! Robert, please don't go! I——' She stopped, embarrassed, both by her words and her erotic thoughts. For a moment she had forgotten the divide between them, but Robert obviously hadn't, because he raised a brow, his eyes mocking her.

'You mustn't call me Robert, my dear. Someone might hear you and you'll have those old tabbies hauling you over the coals again!'

Carrie nodded, her face flushed, her eyes over-bright. Yet somehow she got a grip on herself. Here she was, wishing Robert would make passionate love to her, while her aunt had only just died. 'What—what about Aunt Moira? She arrested, I suppose?'

He nodded, his eyes cold, a man obviously in control of himself once more. 'She had a cardiac arrest soon after you left ITU. Two, in fact. They resuscitated, of course, but. . .' Robert hesitated. 'She'd had angina for a long time. Charles knew about it, told her to slow down, but she wouldn't listen. Her GP knew but your aunt refused medication. She had been running around getting ready for the hospital bazaar, taking on too much, and vigorously resisting help, I should imagine.'

Robert moved nearer, but Carrie backed away, then felt the hard edge of the bed behind her. Whatever happened, Robert mustn't take her in his arms again.

'Your aunt could have gone at any time, Carrie,' the surgeon went on slowly. 'You didn't know?'

'No, I didn't. She never said she was ill.' Poor Aunt Moira. 'I'd better get over to see Uncle Charles. I——' Belatedly Carrie remembered Judy, who would want cheering up. Judy and her world seemed very far away at present, and suddenly Carrie longed to be part of it, longed to be away from death and illness, temperatures, dressings, operations. Wearily she shook her head, not knowing quite *what* she wanted.

'Thank you for coming over to tell me, sir,' she said steadily, meeting his gaze, her youthful pride coming to her rescue. She mustn't let him see how she loved him, for that way lay unhappiness. Her dreams were broken, yet she would always have this one moment to remember, and she could still feel the warmth of his kisses on her mouth.

That mouth trembled now, despite her resolve, and Robert Sheraton's dark gaze softened. He put out a hand as if he would touch her, then withdrew it, with a sigh. 'Poor Carrie. I'd better get back—my aunt and Sarah will be wanting to know what happened. I'm sorry about your weekend. Sorry about everything' he added. 'Be good.' Gently he flicked a finger against her cheek, then he was gone, and she was alone again.

Carrie shivered. Robert was gone and she was alone. And Uncle Charles would be needing her tender loving care. At least she could be of some use to him.

The night air was chilly, a damp chilliness which penetrated every fold of her clothing, and Carrie felt she would never be warm again.

Uncle Charles wasn't in ITU, he was in Robert's office in the annexe, and Carrie had to retrace her steps, leaving the main hospital and crossing the car park towards the annexe, which was completely in darkness except for the light in the surgeon's office. She didn't want to see him again, afraid that even her uncle would sense the love she felt for Robert.

'Judy!' Carrie stopped in the open doorway of the office, her surprised gaze meeting that of her sister, a Judy almost invisible in a multi-caped coat, her long hair trailing over her shoulders.

'Hi, Carrie!' Judy greeted her, then bent her head again to her uncle, who was sitting, just staring into space. Robert stood over by his desk, his gaze sombre as it rested upon Judy and the older man.

Carrie tried desperately to be glad that Judy had arrived to comfort Uncle Charles. 'I'm back again, Uncle. I just went back to my room to change——' Carrie faltered to a halt, but her uncle glanced up and managed a wan smile. 'There wasn't anything you could have done, my pet. Don't worry about it.' Absently he patted her hand, and Judy chimed in.

'Of course you couldn't have saved her, Carrie! Don't start getting a guilt complex, will you? You did your best,' she went on warmly, and Carrie rather wished she would shut up.

She sat down beside their uncle, and took his hand. Their eyes met, Carrie's silent sympathy communicating itself to him. They left Judy and Robert to carry on a hushed conversation, and in her sister's voice Carrie heard what she had heard so often before—what she thought of as the siren sound. Judy was attracted to him and was letting him know it. Poor Robert Sheraton stood no chance at all.

It felt strange, later, going back to Merehurst, driving out into the deep darkness of the night. Uncle Charles had elected to return to his own home for what remained of the night, and when Carrie had remonstrated with him he had merely said he needed to be alone.

Carrie had understood, but Judy had kept begging him to come with them to Merehurst, for Robert had extended an invitation to her to spend the weekend there, and for Carrie to resume her stay. Their uncle had stubbornly resisted all their attempts, and Robert had taken him home before turning off on to the narrow country road which led to Merehurst.

Carrie sat at the back of the car, keeping her own vigil in her heart, while Judy had become the life and soul of the party in the front. She and Robert Sheraton were getting on remarkably well, Carrie noted, and was glad. She didn't feel like holding a conversation, it was too much effort, and the dull ache in her heart wouldn't give her any peace.

'Never mind, Carrie. Don't let it get you down,' Robert said suddenly, and only Carrie knew to what he was referring. How could he treat her love so casually? A teenage infatuation, that was obviously how he regarded it.

She had noted that Judy had called the surgeon by his first name, but that was just Judy's casual way. Carrie was more than surprised, though, when her sister said, with a tinkling laugh, 'You must pop in to see me when you're up in London, Robert. I'd love to show you around. You might meet my father, *our* father. He's big in TV now.'

'Is he? I'm glad to hear it,' the surgeon commented mildly, and Carrie stifled a giggle. She had heard that dry tone before, usually when one of his students had tried to impress with a display of knowledge!

Judy went on, all unaware, 'Yes, he's in great demand—you wouldn't believe it! The two of us vie with each other, you know. It's a bit of fun, but it keeps us on our toes! Isn't that right, Carrie, love? Daddy and I are wild media people, and you're the only one who's sane and sensible. But perhaps once you've qualified you might be interested in joining us in London?'

'I'm sure Nurse West is happy where she is,' Robert said smoothly, as he turned the car through the gates of Merehurst. 'She's doing a worthwhile job and she's doing it well—very well. No one can ask more of life than that. I doubt if the frenetic world of TV appeals to her. It certainly doesn't to me,' he emphasised, and Judy fell silent, while Carrie smiled into the darkness. He thought she was worthwhile!

Ella was sitting up waiting for them. There were dark rings under her eyes, and Carrie scolded her gently. 'You ought to be in bed, Ella! Come on, I'll come up with you.' Linking her arm in the girl's, Carrie led her upstairs, Ella going with her so meekly that the surgeon called after them,

'You ought to be a nanny, Nurse West! You have a commanding way with you.'

Carrie paused halfway up the stairs, and glanced down into the round hallway. Judy was standing very close to the surgeon, gazing at him with a proprietorial air, and Carrie smiled grimly to herself. She continued on her way, leaving Robert to entertain Judy.

She wondered briefly how Judy would entertain *him*, and how long they would stay downstairs talking, then she dismissed the thought. To be jealous of her own sister would be dreadful, and she had never been jealous before, no matter that Judy was popular and beautiful, no matter that Judy had always stolen her boyfriends. . . But there was no question of Judy stealing Robert Sheraton, Carrie mused as she slowly undressed for bed. He wasn't a boyfriend, he was a senior surgeon, and, as such, had no place in Student Nurse West's life.

She drifted off into an uneasy sleep, and it was daylight when she awoke, to find Ella by her bedside, holding out a tray.

'I thought you were never going to wake up, and I told Daddy you were Sleeping Beauty and had to be

awakened with a kiss, and he snapped at me!' Ella said
with a hurt expression.

'Yes, I imagine he did. Consultants don't kiss student
nurses, even when they're off duty,' Carrie said quickly.
'Anyway, thank you for waking me. Is that my breakfast? I never get breakfast in bed!'

Ella obligingly laid the tray across Carrie's knees. '*I*
supervised Annie and told her how you liked your toast.
She carried it up for me.'

Ella sounded so proud that Carrie laughed. 'Thank
you! I like marmalade; Aunt Moira makes——' She
faltered to a halt, then bit into a slice of toast.

'I don't really like marmalade, but I'll have a slice of
yours, shall I? You won't want two.' Ella reached for the
second slice of toast. 'What's your sister like? Is she
nice, like you? I wish I had a sister,' Ella prattled on.
Then she turned those enormous grey eyes on Carrie.
'You could be my sister, if you liked,' she offered, but
Carrie shook her head. No way!

'If I were, then Mr Sheraton would be my father, and
I've already got a father,' she explained carefully. 'I
expect he thinks one daughter is enough. Judy's six years
older than me, and I'm sure you'll like her. Everyone
does.'

Judy appeared just as Carrie was dressing. 'Whatever
possessed that girl to wake me up? I didn't get to sleep
for ages last night! I need my beauty sleep; it's all right
for you nurses, up at all hours dispensing TLC!' Judy
sank down on to the stool which stood in front of the
dressing-table and peered at herself in the mirror. 'I look
a mess. No wonder, being told to get out of bed or I'd
miss breakfast. I never eat breakfast, you know that,'
she went on, and Carrie smiled to herself. Evidently Ella
had seen to it that the luxury of breakfast on a tray
hadn't been extended to Judy!

'Ella and I thought you wanted to be up and doing.
You'll want to meet the rest of the household, won't

you? What are you going to wear? Oh, you haven't any clothes here!'

'Oh, Robert arranged all that. I've got one or two things, just enough for the rest of the weekend. What day is it? Saturday? It seems years since Friday night, doesn't it?' Judy turned to face her. 'We ought to go back to stay with Uncle Charles, don't you think?'

Surprised and touched by Judy's concern for their uncle, Carrie agreed. 'Yes, he might *say* he wants to be alone, and of course we wouldn't disturb him, but it can't be good——'

'*You* wouldn't disturb him, but *I* would,' Judy put in firmly. 'You're a nurse, you understand bereavement. No, I think you're right, you ought to go back to stay with him, soothe his fevered brow, and I'll hang on here until Monday.' She turned back to the mirror, examining her finely marked brows. 'I should have brought my tweezers, there's a stray hair. Have you got yours?'

Carrie shook her head, not trusting herself to speak.

'Oh, well, it doesn't matter. Look, you go back and stay with Uncle Charles and I'll make it all right with Robert's aunt. He'll understand that you feel it's your duty. Doctors understand about duty.'

'Yes, so they do. I thought you wanted to come back with me?' Carrie said unsteadily, but Judy shook her head.

'No, I told you, I would only be in the way, say the wrong thing, perhaps. I'll get dressed and do your packing for you while you're telling them, shall I?'

Carrie managed to match Judy's brilliant smile, though it was an effort. 'I'll ask Mr Sheraton and Aunt Aggie if they mind my leaving,' she conceded. She kept the smile pinned to her face until Judy had made her languid way out of the room.

Good old Nurse West! Well, Judy was right, that was the annoying part. Uncle Charles needed one of them and it wasn't Judy.

When at length Carrie tracked Robert Sheraton down

he was in the conservatory, standing by the door that led down into the garden. He was gazing at nothing in particular, or so it seemed, and his glance was brooding as it rested upon Carrie's flushed face.

'I'm sorry, have I disturbed you?' she asked politely, and he gave a half-smile.

'Yes, you do disturb me rather, but it isn't your fault,' he said quietly, and Carrie didn't know what to make of the remark.

'I—we—Judy and I thought about poor Uncle Charles being left alone and we. . .' Carrie stopped and started again, watched with interest by the surgeon. 'I thought about going back to the house and taking care of him. I wouldn't disturb him, not like Judy, and——'

'Did your sister suggest that her presence would disturb him?' Robert asked gently, and when Carrie nodded he shrugged. 'So a vote was taken and it was decided that Nurse West should rush to the rescue. Was that it?' he went on, still in that same quiet, reasoned tone, and again Carrie nodded, wishing she could get her tongue around the words she really wanted to say.

'Perhaps it's for the best,' he agreed, somewhat to her chagrin. But then, he would prefer Judy, wouldn't he? No! She wasn't going to give up without a fight, hand the man over to Judy on a plate, a golden plate, most likely!

The thought of Robert's head being served up on the best dinner service gave Carrie a fit of giggles. It was an emotional release, and once she had started she couldn't stop, the tears of laughter gradually becoming tears of grief, great tearing sobs that threatened to engulf her.

'Carrie, my pet, my darling. . .' She heard the softly spoken words, but they were coming from miles away. Then strong hands gripped her shoulders and shook her gently. 'Carrie, stop it now, you've cried enough. Carrie!'

Carrie gulped down another sob and gazed unseeingly at him. His hands still gripped her upper arms, but she couldn't see him through the haze of tears.

'Here, a nice clean handkerchief.' A hankie was thrust
into Carrie's hand and she began to wipe her eyes, aware
that her face must be red and puffy. Her hair was a
mess, too, she just knew it. If only she could cry prettily!

Then the handkerchief was prised from her fingers,
and Robert himself made a better job of wiping away the
tears. Carrie trembled, her soft mouth quivering, and he
made a sound halfway between a laugh and a groan.

'Carrie—about last night,' he began, but she didn't
want to listen to words of apology. It was more than she
could bear.

'That's quite all right. I understand it was just TLC,'
she said swiftly.

'Oh, Carrie, you're so vulnerable. I wish——' He
stopped, and Carrie opened her eyes wide, then sniffed.

'Thank you for the hankie—I'll wash it and send it
back,' she went on, in a calmer tone. How stupid of her
to cry in front of him. 'I'm all right now, thank you, sir,'
she said coolly. The expression on his face stopped her
from saying more. He looked. . .wretched. Was that the
word? she wondered. Yes, wretched and unhappy. Very,
very unhappy.

Hesitantly she put out a hand to touch his dear face.
'I'm sorry, Robert,' she whispered, and this time he
didn't take her to task for using his Christian name. He
just stood there, evidently fighting an inner battle—and
winning.

'I think you ought to go back now, Carrie. Your
sister's right about that.' Abruptly he turned from her,
resuming his former pose by the door. When he spoke
again, his voice was muffled. 'Don't envy your sister,
Carrie; you have far more to offer than she has. I'll drive
you back—give me a minute or two to change.'

She would have protested but held her tongue,
instead. Yes, she would like him to drive her home.

When she came downstairs again, having had to
repack her belongings since Judy hadn't made much of

a job of it, she met Sarah Nugent in the doorway of Robert's study.

'I hear you're leaving us, Carrie,' she said, manoeuvring herself alongside Carrie.

'Yes, I expect Mr Sheraton explained about my uncle?' At Miss Nugent's quick nod, Carrie went on, 'We thought it best—Judy and I—that I should be the one who went back to stay with him—me being a nurse,' she went on, since the other woman remained silent.

'A busman's holiday for you,' was the only comment Sarah Nugent made. Then she put out her slender hand and squeezed Carrie's. 'It's just as well, my dear. Aunt Aggie doesn't want too many people in the house. I think your sister ought to go home as well. Only. . .' She hesitated, and a feeling of dread settled around Carrie's heart. What was coming next?

'You might wonder what sort of relationship Robert and I have,' Miss Nugent said, after a pause. Carrie made a small gesture that indicated she wasn't the slightest bit interested, but Miss Nugent went on, 'In fact, I'm sure you must have wondered, but it has always been understood that one day Robert and I would——' She broke off, as Ella came hurrying up. Carrie didn't need the sentence completed. It was all too obvious. One day Robert and I would marry.

CHAPTER ELEVEN

ROBERT SHERATON was silent for much of the journey, and Carrie herself didn't want to talk, but at last he broke the heavy, brooding silence. 'I'm sorry your weekend off has turned out so badly, Carrie. I wish things could have been different.' His voice sounded strained, unnatural.

'I wish things had turned out better for Uncle Charles,' Carrie said quietly, 'but Aunt Moira never seemed happy. Of course I didn't know she had all those chest pains, but nothing was ever right for her. It's a dreadful thing to say but perhaps she's at rest now. What I mean is, she——'

'I know exactly what you mean, my dear. Those who suffer most are often the most cheerful,' he added, and Carrie nodded in total agreement.

'Like Miss Nugent,' she said.

'Like Miss Nugent?' Robert prompted, and Carrie had to go on.

'Well, she's in a wheelchair and says she'll never walk again, but I didn't hear her complain. She takes life as it comes, I think.'

'Yes, she does. Sarah's a dear, very kind and helpful,' he went on, and Carrie agreed doubtfully. 'We've known each other for years,' Robert said slowly, his swift glance appraising her. Then he slowed the car and parked in a lay-by.

He turned towards her, Carrie didn't want to hear whatever he had to say.

'Sarah——' He hesitated. 'She was a bit put out when I fell head over heels in love with Mireille—Ella's mother. She got over it, though, and I know she and the local vet have something going. I dare say they'll marry in due course. There's no medical reason why they shouldn't,' he went on, to Carrie's intense relief.

'I thought——' She stopped. Miss Nugent had more or less said she had hopes of marrying the surgeon, but Carrie couldn't betray her confidence. 'I thought she and Ella got on very well,' she said instead, and Robert's smile was quizzical.

'Was that what you were going to say? I don't think so. You're learning to think before you open your mouth now. That's a sign of maturity, Nurse West. And another thing——'

'Why am I Nurse West now?' Carrie demanded bluntly, forgetting that she had decided not to mention the matter. 'I was Carrie before!'

'So you were, but that was then, this is now. On Monday, you will be Student Nurse West again and I shall be Sir, He Who Must Be Obeyed,' he said, with a twinkle in those fine eyes, and Carrie's lips quivered, but she refused to laugh.

'I see. Sir,' she added, and Robert sighed.

'I was about to remark that you haven't tried to give me the benefit of your opinion lately, but I suppose next week you'll think of some way I could be improved,' he said teasingly.

'I shall think of something by Monday, I expect,' she admitted.

Idly, Robert tapped his fingers on the wheel, and Carrie watched them. Long, sensitive fingers, a well-shaped capable hand, a healing hand. . . Then he sighed. 'I'd better get you back. I promised Judy I would take her riding and I've a busy morning ahead of me.'

Judy had never, to Carrie's knowledge, even been on a horse, but she let it pass. She and Robert shared a love of healing, were concerned from day to day in the business of caring for the sick and disabled—that was something Judy could never share.

They didn't speak again, and soon her uncle's house

came into sight, a house that she supposed she ought to think of as 'home' but rarely did.

'Here we are, home sweet home, but I suppose it isn't really?' Robert's words had uncannily echoed her own thoughts, and Carrie shook her head, pinning her 'Cheery Nurse West' smile to her face once more.

'No, it isn't really, but it isn't fair to Uncle Charles and—and Aunt Moira to say that. Perhaps I'll go up to London once I qualify,' she babbled on, anything to prolong this moment. Once she got out of the car, she felt she would never be close to him again, certainly never share this feeling of camaraderie.

'London's streets aren't paved with gold, Carrie,' he said seriously, half turning towards her. 'I know when you're young you think they are. London seems a glamorous, exciting place, full of opportunities, but when you're my age you'll see that it——'

'Will you stop harping on about your age?' she flashed, forgetting that this certainly wasn't the way to talk to a consultant. 'Anyone would think you were a greybeard! I'm not that young, and I do understand about London, or any city, being a lonely place, but there are lots of opportunities for nurses, and I ought to spread my wings a little. 'I've become too parochial.' Parochial was a favourite word of Judy's and Carrie rather resented having it flung at her at intervals, but it probably summed her up. She needed to branch out, see something of the world beyond Sussex and St Hilda's.

'Parochial isn't a word I would use to describe you, Carrie.' There was a smile in Robert's voice. 'But I agree that you need to grasp all those golden opportunities, see the world, perhaps.' He paused, gazing into a future that, judging by his expression, looked a bleak one. 'Yes, you ought to leave St Hilda's once you're trained, spread your wings. . .'

He flicked her cheek with one finger, in that way he had. It was a kindly, almost avuncular gesture, and it broke Carrie's heart. She felt like crying, but would not.

'Oh, Carrie! My dear, dear Carrie!' Her name was a cry of anguish from the surgeon, and she saw that his hands were gripping the steering-wheel as though it were a lifeline, the straw that a drowning man would grasp as he was swept along in the raging torrent to his doom.

'Robert?' Carrie spoke his name softly, tentatively, forgetting that he had told her not to use it. 'Robert, please don't look like that—I can't bear it!'

Forgetting herself again, she stretched up and kissed him gently on the cheek.

There was silence for a moment, and Carrie could almost see him fighting a battle with himself. Then his face took on that distant, autocratic expression—the consultant surgeon looking right through the junior member of staff who had dared to address him, but this time Carrie wasn't fooled. She knew that it was a mask. Even on that first meeting with him, way back before Christmas, it had been a mask, a defence erected to hide the fact that he was a very human man, with a man's weaknesses and strengths. He was no demi-god and she wasn't going to let him retreat behind the mask again.

'You needn't look like that, either,' she said pertly. 'There's no point in telling me I've spoken out of turn or—or done something dreadful, because I know it. And I won't apologise!' She sat back, arms folded defensively.

'I'm not sure what it is I look like,' Robert said after a moment. 'I think you *have* done something dreadful, my pet, but I won't tell you what it is.' He got out of the car and was at the other side, holding the door open for Carrie before she fully recovered her wits. 'Come on, out you get. Charles will be glad to see you, I know. But let him stay by himself if he wants, Carrie. Don't force company on him.'

Robert's smile was tinged with sadness, Carrie thought, and he was about to turn away as she began to thank him for the lift, thank him for his kindness to her and to her uncle and aunt. But she couldn't, wouldn't let him go like that. She stood waiting, *willing* him to

speak just one word of love. Love? No, perhaps not,
but——

He did turn then, his eyes unfathomable. 'I'd like to
kiss you, Carrie, but it would be wrong, and unfair.
Unfair to us both,' he added.

He didn't glance back as he drove slowly off, and
Carrie watched until he was out of sight. Even then, she
didn't go into the house, despite the cold. The cheery
Nurse West wasn't feeling so cheery.

Picking up her overnight bag, she moved at last, her
feet crunching on the gravel path that led to her uncle's
door. Goodbye, Robert, she said silently.

Monday morning brought a return to harsh reality, the
weekend becoming part of a dream. Sister Carter was
still off sick, but the relief sister, Edna Marchant, was a
real tartar, and she was in a picky mood. Carrie fell foul
of her on several occasions. Sister Carter she could cope
with but no one could cope with Sister Marchant on the
warpath!

She had to admit that one or two of the sister's
criticisms were justified, though. Whenever she had a
spare moment, and sometimes when she didn't, Carrie
found herself daydreaming, wondering what life with
Robert would be like. She would make him *so* happy,
she knew she would! That dreadful, tense, cold-eyed
look would disappear, and she would make him laugh.
Help Ella, too. Then there was Aunt Aggie and Uncle
Charles. And Miss Nugent. . . Yes, don't forget Miss
Nugent, she thought, the happy bubble vanishing.
Despite what Robert had said, Sarah Nugent seemed to
think she had sole rights to him. Then there was
Judy. . .

Unbelievably, Judy was staying on with Aunt Aggie!
Carrie could recall her sister's phone call on Sunday
evening, almost word for word. Ella's great-aunt was
rather a pet, and Miss Nugent had been quite pleasant,
but Robert! Ah, Robert was an absolute stunner! Didn't

Carrie think so? But of course Carrie would think him rather on the old side, but really he was utterly charming. Oh, and Daddy had phoned to say he would be coming down for Aunt Moira's funeral. They must all have dinner together soon, and Robert, naturally. Carrie would enjoy that, wouldn't she?

Without waiting for Carrie's less than enthusiastic response, Judy had rung off, and Carrie had been left holding the receiver.

Shrugging aside her unhappiness, Carrie got the suture-removing pack ready for Mrs Duncan, who was due to have half her sutures removed.

'Staff will be along in a minute, Mrs Duncan,' she said, moments later, as she smiled down at the woman. 'Then we'll take them out together. There's nothing to worry about.' Sister Carter would have left Carrie to do the job, knowing she could be trusted to follow a strict aseptic technique, but Sister Marchant must make her own rules, and trusting students wasn't one of them!

Carrie smiled to herself as she whisked the curtains around the bed. She had never thought she would be glad to see the return of Sister Carter, but that day had dawned.

'We'll soon have——' she began, then some sixth sense told her that Robert Sheraton was on the ward. She hesitated, wanting above all things to peek out of the curtains, but that would be unprofessional. On the other hand, if she didn't, she wouldn't know when Staff was ready. So, having convinced herself that she had a good excuse, Carrie stuck her head out from the curtained-off bed—to meet the far from friendly gaze of the man himself.

'Good morning, sir,' she said crisply, recovering instantly. She had made a belated New Year's Resolution: whatever happened, she would keep her cool, behave exactly as any other junior nurse would to a consultant. She would treat him with the respect that his station deserved. She wouldn't trouble him with her opinion, since consultants didn't think nurses *had* opinions. Of course, on the other hand, she wouldn't toad-eat him or——

Suddenly aware that she was staring at the man, Carrie hastily withdrew her head. Outside the curtain she was almost sure she heard that throaty chuckle, but she knew she must be mistaken. Mr Sheraton would never laugh at anything she said or did again. There, she had taken to calling him 'Mr Sheraton' even in her own mind!

Recalling herself to her patient, she said briskly, 'I think Staff Nurse is busy just now, so I'll just pop out and see how long she'll be. All right if I leave the curtains drawn?'

'Yes, I'd like that, Nurse Carrie. Give me a bit of privacy. It won't hurt, taking out them stitches, will it?' she asked, just as Carrie was about to slip out through the curtains.

Carrie was about to reassure her, but unfortunately the question had distracted her attention, and she backed into a large, immovable body. 'I——Oh, I'm sorry!' Fortunately it wasn't the surgeon, but the large Sister Marchant was only slightly better.

'What *are* you doing, Nurse West? No, don't tell me now. I shall see you in my office, later,' Sister said, not giving Carrie a chance to open her mouth. Robert Sheraton's lips twitched slightly and he turned away, obviously to hide his smile from Sister. Now even *he* was laughing at her!

'Yes, Sister. Sorry, Sister,' Carrie mumbled the time-honoured words. 'I was looking for Staff, Sister. Shall I——?'

'*I* will superintend the removal of the sutures shortly, Nurse. Find yourself something to do, and open—those—curtains.' This last instruction was spoken slowly and distinctly, and Carrie's temper rose.

'Mrs Duncan is happy with the curtains closed, please, Sister. I'll only be a minute.' Head held high, Carrie sped away with her quick nurse's walk, the lump in her throat leading her to believe that she was sickening for the very same bug that had left Sister Carter feeling so low. It would serve Sister Marchant right if she went off sick!

With that unerring instinct common to all learner nurses, Carrie made for the linen cupboard. One thing she missed and that was the sight of Ann Haynes crying into the spare sheets. For the next few days Ann was on late duty and Carrie missed her companionship, even though Ann's lacrymose ways were a trial at times.

Well, if Ann cried again she would have more sympathy with her, for there was nothing she herself wanted more than to bury her head in the linen and howl the place down!

Love, Carrie decided, wasn't all it was cracked up to be.

The interview with Sister Marchant, much later, wasn't as bad as Carrie had feared, or perhaps it was that by then she had a far greater burden to bear, and the sister's harsh words simply passed over her head. For, to her horror, Carrie found that Robert Sheraton, once known as 'Sensuous Sheraton', had been given a new nickname—'Caroline's Conquest'!

Carrie stared at the second-year who had eagerly imparted this information. 'Caroline's Conquest?' Carrie echoed. 'What on earth for? I know I spent part of the weekend there but Sister Carter was supposed to go, too. It isn't my fault she went sick! I didn't sabotage her drinking water,' she went on acidly, in case her displeasure wasn't obvious to the girl.

'Of course you didn't! But it's all round the hospital, Carrie. *He* only invited Sister because he couldn't invite you by yourself. When he knew Sister was ill, he ought to have cancelled your visit, but he didn't, did he? No,' the student went on relentlessly, 'that's because he wanted you all to himself!'

'He didn't have me all to himself,' Carrie said firmly.

'Because Sister couldn't come, he invited my Aunt Moira instead—Dr Warriner's wife. And there was another guest in the house, plus his daughter and his aunt.'

'But why would he ask you in the first place?'

To that question there seemed no answer, but Carrie tried, anyway. Unfortunately, she hesitated before she spoke, and a knowing grin appeared on the face of her assailant, for that was how Carrie thought of her. 'Ella—that's his daughter—didn't have anyone to stay with her and she gets lonely and——'

'That explanation won't wash, Carrie, and you know it! The man's crazy about you. I've seen him look at you,' the student went on, a trifle wistfully, Carrie thought.

'He was probably looking through me rather than *at* me. You know what consultants are like,' Carrie said crisply. 'Anyway, when we go into block, this silly name will be forgotten. When I go back to the wards, it will be Men's Medical and I shan't see *him* there, so you're spreading malicious gossip for nothing, aren't you?' With that parting shot, Carrie walked away from the girl, quietly fuming. How dared they? If that name should get back to Robert. . .

It was several days before the remark reached him, and by that time Sister Carter was back on the ward. She questioned Carrie closely about her aborted stay with Robert's aunt, expressed her sympathy at Aunt Moira's death, then put in, casually, just as a relieved Carrie was about to return to the ward, that she was dining with Robert Sheraton that evening.

'He said how sorry he was that I couldn't go for the weekend, so it might be——' Sister broke off suddenly, as if belatedly remembering that she shouldn't be discussing her private life with a learner. 'Off you go, Nurse West. And do try to be more professional! Sister Marchant was full of complaints about you. I know——' She held up a hand as Carrie was about to launch into the attack. 'I know, but you are a bit slapdash sometimes. A little more thought and you'll be well on the way to becoming a valued member of the ward team. You have the makings of a fine nurse,' she added generously.

'Yes, Sister. Thank you, Sister,' Carrie said in surprise, then edged her way out of the door, wondering how long Sister's genial mood would last. No doubt until she discovered that Robert was seeing a lot of Nurse West's elder sister!

The funeral was private, and Robert didn't attend it, but many of Dr Warriner's colleagues and friends joined the family at the house afterwards, and Carrie was glad to see that Robert Sheraton was among their number. She wouldn't have thought the house could hold so many, and knew how chuffed her uncle must be by the presence of so many old friends. Judy, Carrie noted with approval, had put herself out and was acting as hostess, seeing that even the quietest person was perfectly at ease.

Right at this moment, the person Judy was looking after was Robert, for she hadn't budged from his side for at least ten minutes, Carrie herself having to carry on conversations with people much senior to her, some of whom she had done no more than glimpse in the hospital. Carrie sighed, wondering whether she could escape into the kitchen, and begin the washing-up. It wasn't likely anyone would miss her for a while, at least. She couldn't help wondering where her father was, though, for he hadn't turned up for his sister-in-law's funeral.

She was beginning on the washing-up when her uncle appeared in the kitchen doorway. 'There you are! I asked Judy and she said she thought you had gone to your room.'

'I know Mrs Cullen's coming in later, but I thought I would just make a start on the dishes,' Carrie explained. 'Can I make you a nice cup of tea? There's nothing like a cuppa,' she said cheerily, then remembered that she wasn't speaking to a patient.

'Nothing I'd like better, my pet. Thank you.' He sat down at the kitchen table, and Carrie peeled off her washing-up gloves. Then she saw the box her uncle was holding out and her eyes widened.

'Put the kettle on, Carrie, and come and look at these. Your aunt wanted you to have them and I've been trying to get you on your own.'

Surprised, Carrie did as she was bidden. She recognised the box, or rather the jewel case. It held Aunt Moira's precious pearl necklace. She didn't know if the pearls were real, but they had been her aunt's pride and joy, and brought out only on special occasions. Surely they weren't for her?

They were. Carrie opened the case and gazed down at the pearls, which seemed to shimmer before her eyes. Perhaps that was because she was viewing them through a veil of tears. 'They can't be for me! Surely Judy should have them. Aunt Moira liked Judy better,' Carrie said diffidently.

'Yes, I suppose she did. You were always such a harum-scarum child, and Judy was so neat and tidy.' Uncle Charles shrugged. 'Judy was older, of course, not really a child at all, and Moira didn't like children. But she knew I had a soft spot for you, and she once told me that if anything happened to her you were to have the pearls. She thought you would probably be of an age to value them by the time you inherited, but—anyway, take care of them, and don't leave them in the nurses' home. You might, if you wished, leave them with me and I'll bring them out for you to wear on special occasions, just like Moira. You know where she kept them. How about that?'

Carrie nodded, too full to speak. Then she ran across and hugged her uncle. 'Thank you! I'll treasure them always, and I promise I *will* take care of them. But—are you sure? I know Aunt Moira valued them and. . .'

Carrie hesitated. 'They're part of her, really, aren't they? I don't want to part you from them and——'

Her uncle's eyes were moist as he gazed at her. 'I have my memories, Carrie. No one can take those from me. I have memories of Moira when we were young. She was different then, you know. You wouldn't have recognised her. Pain can change people's personalities. She never really recovered from her mother's death, then your mother died and one of her friends from schooldays. She found it difficult to cope. Then the angina started and she threw herself into 'do-gooding'. In an attempt to shut out mental as well as physical pain, I suppose. Nothing *I* said had any influence on her. No, you take the pearls, my dear.'

Absently he stroked Carrie's hair, and she leaned against him for a moment, wishing *he* was her father. 'What about Judy?' she whispered. 'She ought to have something.'

'Well, don't offer her the pearls! Why should you? I dare say there will be something of Moira's I can give her,' he went on firmly.

Stunned and not really believing her good fortune, Carrie made the tea, her hands trembling slightly.

Then there was a tap on the kitchen door, and a tall, spare man pushed the door open. Dad! Carrie opened her mouth once again, then closed it, for behind her father came the equally tall form of Robert Sheraton.

The pearls still lay in their open case, and her father whistled when he saw them. 'Moira's famous pearl necklace! Not going to give the pearls to this little cherub, are you, Charles? She'll lose them—won't you, Carrie?'

'No,' Carrie said slowly and deliberately. 'I promise to take care of them. Thank you, Uncle Charles.' She closed the case, paused to brush her father's cheek with her lips, then hurried away, determined to replace the jewels in the cupboard where her aunt had always kept them. Although the cupboard wasn't locked, it had a

secret drawer, and only her uncle and aunt, she and
Judy knew how it worked. They would be safe there.

Robert was waiting for her in the kitchen when she
returned, both her father and uncle having joined the
guests. Carrie paused, eyeing him dubiously. There was
a look in his eyes that boded ill for somebody, probably
herself.

'Did you want to tell me something, sir?' she asked
softly, then heard his sharp intake of breath.

'Sometimes I do,' he said cryptically, 'but this isn't
the time or the place, Nurse West. I'll see you on the
ward some time—if I dare put in an appearance there
again,' he added tautly.

Carrie put a hand to her mouth. He knew—Caroline's
Conquest knew!

The last day of her stint on Marigold Ward came around
before she knew it. There would be a long weekend off,
then into study block. No more Marigold Ward with its
cheerful atmosphere, its friendly patients, its gorgeous
consultant——

Then Staff Nurse handed her a message, and Carrie
snapped out of her daydream. She was wanted in Mr
Sheraton's office!

Well, she knew what *that* would be about! But it
wasn't the end of the world. Robert would simply give
her a dressing-down, but he couldn't eat her! Anyway,
the nickname wasn't her fault, he would surely realise
that. Why, they might end up having a good laugh about
it.

Then again, they might not, Carrie thought gloomily
a few minutes later as she and the staff nurse settled the
new patient into the ward. The dreaded appointment
wasn't for another hour, so there was plenty of time for
attending to the new lady, Mrs Pilcher. At least Carrie
hoped there was. It wouldn't do to be late for the
appointment, or confrontation, and Robert wouldn't

accept the excuse that patients came first. Well, he would have to!

'Don't frown at our new patient, Nurse West. You'll have her thinking we don't want her with us!'

'I wish I *wasn't* with you!' Mrs Pilcher admitted, with a nervous giggle, and Carrie beamed at her.

'I didn't mean to frown, Mrs Pilcher. It's my last day on Marigold, so I'll try to make you feel welcome.' As she spoke, Carrie was helping to unfold the bedclothes, which had been made up into a pack as it was an admission bed.

Norah Pilcher was thirty-nine, a married woman with three children, and had been admitted for an abdominal hysterectomy, after several months of out-patient treatment. Her husband, who looked a lot older than his wife, was hovering just outside the bed curtains, and Carrie would have invited him to sit in the visitors' room with a cup of tea and a magazine until Sister had time to talk to him, but he had insisted on remaining where he was. It was important to make the relative feel he or she was needed, so no one tried to persuade Mr Pilcher to move.

Once his wife was in bed, Mr Pilcher was told he could come into the cubicle, and Carrie and the staff nurse left them alone for a few minutes. Later, Mrs Pilcher would be introduced to her bed neighbours, only two at present since they actually had a vacancy until the afternoon. The other two were in the dayroom so the Pilchers could have a little privacy—something in short supply in hospital wards.

Before Mr Pilcher left, Sister Carter would see him, while a nurse attended to his wife, taking care of her clothing, and giving her any information she might need. It wouldn't be Carrie's turn to give out the questionnaire. Another nurse would be Mrs Pilcher's 'own' nurse and Carrie was sorry. She had taken to the tall, nervous lady straight away and genuinely wished she could help her. Never mind, she would have time for a chat before

leaving Marigold—*after* the interview with Caroline's
Conquest!

Get the apology in first, she told herself, take the wind
out of his sails. It was simple really.

It wasn't so simple once she was standing in front of
his desk. This time there was no staff nurse in his room;
there were just the two of them. 'If it's about that
dreadful nickname,' she began, intending to apologise
straight away, 'I'm——'

'You are what, Nurse West? Sorry you boasted about
your conquest?' His tone was biting, his lips set in a
harsh line. 'Couldn't you wait at least until you left
gynae? Did you have to start boasting the minute you
were invited for the weekend? When I came back here,
and one of my *senior* colleagues slapped me on the back
and said he'd never enjoyed a joke so much in years, I
could have sunk through the floor!'

'That's just how *I* feel when you're being angry and
unreasonable!' Carrie flung at him, glad that the door
was closed and they could have a good old slanging
match. It was time someone told Mr Robert Sheraton a
few home truths!

'Am I unreasonable? Of course I'm not.' Robert waved
away such an outrageous suggestion, but Carrie wasn't
going to let him get away with that.

'You're like a bear with a sore head most mornings,'
she said tartly, 'and another thing——'

'Yes, Nurse West?' The anger had died, at least on
the surface, but his voice was cold steel, and Carrie
hesitated. Most learners would never dream of talking to
a surgeon like that, not even a registrar, but this man
was a consultant. Still, it needed saying and she was
never one to dodge an issue.

'You're always picking holes in me, in my work, in
what I do in my leisure time. Then you saw Judy
and——'

'Aha!' He sat back in his swivel chair, an annoying
little smile playing about his mouth. 'Go on, Nurse, this

is becoming interesting.' He almost purred the words. He was enjoying a joke at her expense; that much was obvious.

'Every time something goes wrong on Marigold, *I* get the blame,' she said stubbornly, knowing that it wasn't quite true, but it was near enough. 'You haven't a kind word to say to me and you won't listen when I try to explain! *I* didn't call you "Caroline's Conquest". *I* never mentioned you.' Aggrieved, she perched on the edge of the chair opposite him, her green gaze willing him to understand. With understanding came forgiveness, or so she had read in her psychology book.

Evidently he hadn't read the same book, for those dark brows drew together in a frown. 'I shall overlook the fact that you are being exceedingly rude, Nurse. But you must be responsible for that odious nickname! Who else but you could have told your bosom friends that you were joining me for the weekend? I'm sure Sister Carter never said anything.'

Carrie silently agreed. No, it couldn't have come from Sister, but who, except herself and Uncle Charles, knew? 'No, it couldn't have been her, sir, but——'

'I'm "sir" now, am I? You were rather less polite a moment ago,' Robert observed quietly, and Carrie looked down at her hands. Her fists were clenched, a sure give-away in psychology books. Hurriedly, she unclenched them.

'You don't like me,' she observed, 'and I'm sorry, but I *do* try. I like nursing and I'm not going to leave, no matter how much you make my life a misery!' She glanced up again, her eyes flashing.

'I wasn't aware I made your life a misery, Carrie, but you surely make *mine* a misery sometimes. No, more than sometimes,' he mused, half to himself.

'Me? I mean, *I* do?'

He waved her to silence. 'Yes, you, Nurse Caroline West. I prefer your sister, you know. At least *she* doesn't irritate me, aggravate me at every opportunity, tell me I'm like a bear with a sore head, a——'

'You aren't *always* like that,' Carrie said, trying to be fair, and the surgeon choked back what might have been a laugh.

'I suggest you go and offer my patients plenty of TLC, Nurse,' he said, after a moment, and Carrie rose.

'It's my last day on your ward, sir, so I'll say goodbye. You won't be seeing me again.' With that, Carrie spun on her heel and marched to the door. She would never see him again, except in the distance, and she didn't care. At least, she tried to tell herself that she didn't.

If she expected him to call her back, tell her he was sorry she was going, then she was to be disappointed. Instead, he said, 'I'm glad you're leaving Marigold, Nurse West. I really am.'

CHAPTER TWELVE

SCHOOL was horribly dull after Marigold Ward, and Carrie missed the hustle and bustle of a busy surgical ward, missed the patients, missed the consultant. . .

Despite pining for Robert, she had accepted an invitation from Terry, the medical student whose open adoration went some way towards soothing her feelings. Tonight they were painting the town red, though Carrie knew it would be *her* money they would use for painting, since medics had very little to live on, or so Terry assured her as he borrowed a few pounds yet again.

Nurses were badly paid as well, yet Robert Sheraton had all that money. As for Aunt Aggie's house. . . Why, it was a mansion! 'Unto every one that hath shall be given' Carrie thought, as the lecture broke up. Quite what it had been about, she wasn't sure.

Robert had enjoyed an easy life, but what about poor Eileen Jordan? Carrie was particularly upset about her, for she had met the ex-patient only yesterday. The poor woman still had nowhere to go, though, as Ann had said, the Council had found her temporary accommodation. Robert's aunt could have housed ten Eileen Jordans and still that mansion would have been under-occupied.

Still brooding on the injustice of it all, she didn't at first notice the consultant. But she heard a low, musical laugh she recognised all too well—Judy!

Glancing about her in surprise, Carrie finally located her sister by the side-door which led out to the admin block. Judy and Robert Sheraton, deep in conversation, and from the absorbed expression on Robert's face he was enjoying himself.

Then Judy half turned, her face alight, though Carrie noted that it clouded slightly when she saw her. Judy waved, though, and Carrie had no option but to cross over to them, her textbooks clutched defensively to her small breasts.

In her uniform, so practical but dull, she felt at a disadvantage. Judy was wearing a culotte suit of grey and white check, and looked superb. But then she always did.

'Hello, pet!' Judy leaned forward and pecked her on the cheek. 'You're looking very professional and efficient. Isn't she, Robert?' That brilliant, irresistible smile was turned upon the surgeon, who nodded, his expression enigmatic as he glanced towards Carrie. 'Glanced' was about all he did, for he seemed abstracted, and Carrie got the idea that he wasn't really seeing her, that there was something more pressing on his mind. Probably wondering how quickly he could get Judy in his bed, she thought, then flushed as Judy continued to stare at her.

'Nursing isn't sending you deaf, is it, Carrie? I asked whether you would like to have lunch with us. We're lunching in the consultants' dining-room,' Judy confided, 'but I'm sure Robert won't mind one extra.' She laid a hand on his arm and he looked vaguely discomfited, as well he might, since they were in full view of anyone walking by. It being lunchtime, everyone *was* walking by, and some were pausing to glance over at the trio.

'I'm afraid students aren't allowed in the consultants' dining-room, Judy. But thank you, anyway.' Carrie hesitated. She really wanted to tell Robert about Mrs Jordan and she might not get another chance. It wasn't as if she would ever see him on the ward again. 'Excuse me, sir, but could I just tell you about Eileen Jordan? She was one of your patients,' she hurried on as Robert looked blank.

'Ah, yes, Eileen Jordan. Yes, what about her?' He stood there, his gaze sad, and Carrie had the absurd desire to reach out and stroke his face, tease him into a smile. The thought made her flush even more, and she stood first on one foot then on the other, until Judy giggled.

'Oh, Carrie, you're blushing! There's no need, Robert won't eat you. Go ahead, pet, I promise to protect you from the big, bad consultant surgeon!'

Judy was making it a thousand times worse, and she couldn't have done more harm if she had tried deliberately to embarrass her. Of course Judy wouldn't do a thing like that, and Carrie hastily dismissed the disloyal thought.

Robert himself came to Carrie's rescue, just as she had decided to smile, murmur that it wasn't important, and walk on. 'I'll walk a little way with Nurse West, Judy. Why don't you make yourself comfortable in the consultants' common-room? It's the second door along on the left.' Robert smiled winningly at Judy, who pouted.

'Oh, must I? You won't be long, though, will you? See you, Carrie! Oh, by the way, I wondered if I could— no, never mind. I'll ask you later.' Judy tottered away on very high heels, Robert's eyes following her.

'Now, Nurse West—what's this about Mrs Jordan? Have you seen her lately?'

He did remember her, then! Feeling absurdly pleased because he hadn't forgotten the patient, Carrie launched into her prepared speech about Mrs Jordan's housing problem, her husband's bad chest, the fact that some people lived in big houses while others had trouble finding even one room. She didn't mean to mention his own circumstances, or those of his aunt, but somehow it all came out. 'She hasn't *anywhere* to go, sir, and there are people with lots and lots of room. It's so unfair!'

'I agree, Nurse West, it's very unfair,' he put in mildly, once she had ground to a halt. 'Perhaps we should start a revolution? Hm? Send all the aristocracy to the salt mines and redistribute their land and wealth. How would that be? I vote that Nurse Caroline West becomes Prime Minister. Down with the landed gentry

and consultants who have too much money! How is that
for a slogan?'

His sarcasm was worse than his evil temper. 'There's
no need to be sarcastic, sir! It's just so rotten that Mrs
Jordan hasn't got anywhere. You know she isn't well
and then there's the ——'

Robert held up a hand. 'Please don't launch into
another chapter of the woman's problems, Nurse. She
has, at least, been rehoused somewhere. She isn't home-
less, living under the railway arches or stretched out on
a park bench,' he pointed out acidly, and Carrie's face
darkened. He didn't care, he wasn't the slightest bit
interested in other people's problems.

'I apologise for troubling you, Mr Sheraton,' she said
coldly, her small face grim and set. 'I should have
realised that as *you* live in a big house you couldn't
possibly understand the problems of people who haven't
enough money to buy even a small flat. Goodbye, sir.'

She walked stiffly away, every muscle aching, including her heart. That Robert might not understand, she
could accept, but that he might not even care about the
Mrs Jordans of this world she could never forgive.

The disco was over-loud, the lights too bright, and
Carrie was glad when Terry Hammond suggested they
leave early. Quite where they would go she wasn't sure.
One thing *was* for sure—if Terry thought he was about
to enjoy a romantic interlude he was in for a rude
awakening!

He beamed at her in the light from the street-lamp
outside the disco. 'Wasn't that great—brill! It got a bit
stuffy in there, though. Wheee!' He executed a little
dance around the lamp-post and Carrie eyed him
askance.

Then, before she could suggest sharing a taxi back to
St Hilda's, he stopped dancing and took her in his arms.
'You know, you really are the loveliest creature, Carrie.

I don't mind a bit if the old man's called Caroline's Conquest. *I* want to be Caroline's Conquest!'

She managed, with difficulty, to extricate herself, then began to walk away, but Terry came lumbering after her and swept her into his arms again the very moment that Robert Sheraton and Judy passed by in Robert's car. Carrie had to suffer a kiss she didn't want and hadn't encouraged, then, before she could hide her face, Judy had hailed her, and a flustered Carrie waved, before turning to her escort. 'Thanks to you, my sister saw us! If you hadn't behaved like that, she wouldn't have noticed either of us!'

'What you mean is, *he* wouldn't have noticed either of us!' Terry's remark was too near the truth and Carrie fell silent.

'That's right, sulk!' Terry went on. 'I'm sorry if I've spoiled whatever you and that guy have got going, but you shouldn't have——'

'What should Nurse West not have done?' a cool voice broke in, and Carrie's face burned.

'Oh, hello, sir!' Terry was almost ready to tug his forelock, Carrie thought resentfully, but it wasn't Terry who would feel the full force of Robert Sheraton's sharp tongue.

'Good evening, sir,' Carrie chanted. 'Terry and I have just been to the disco. There's lots of St Hilda's people there. Are you going?'

Then Judy strolled up, linking her arm through the surgeon's. 'We're off to the Inn on the Sidewalk, but Robert thought he saw a girl being attacked in front of the disco so we had to stop, and it turned out to be you, enjoying a really good kiss by the looks of it!'

'Since you seem to be able to take care of yourself, Nurse, I'll be getting along.' Robert's voice was cold. 'Oh, by the way, Ella wants you to come for tea one day. Shall I tell her you'll give her a ring before she goes back to school?'

'Oh, yes! Thank you, sir. I'll do that. Is she all right?'

Carrie asked, glad that they were no longer discussing the unwanted kiss.

'Full of beans and getting up to all sorts of mischief,' Ella's father said drily. 'Anyway, ring her tomorrow—if you have time.'

Then he went, Judy struggling to keep up with his stride. Carrie rather enjoyed watching her sister run to keep up with the man they both loved.

Robert and Judy had crossed the road again before Carrie came to her senses. No! She couldn't leave it like that, she had to explain. . . How she was to explain the seemingly passionate embrace, she wasn't sure, but she meant to try.

Without thinking and with only a cursory glance to right and left, Carrie darted across the street and didn't see the car until it was too late. . .

Moments later, she came to, dimly aware of voices, lights, particularly a flashing blue light. Then she closed her eyes again. She was so terribly tired and she did *so* want to tell Robert that she cared nothing for Terry. 'Robert,' she murmured. The name echoed in her dreams, or perhaps it was reality. Whatever it was, she felt herself drifting along a slow, torpid river. She was quite alone, with only Robert's name to guide her.

Then she heard her own name, quite distinctly. 'Caroline,' a voice said. 'Carrie, wake up!'

It was a command and she tried to obey, but she had reached a whirlpool in the river now and she was caught up in it. 'Carrie!' The familiar voice penetrated, the whirlpool dissolved, and Carrie tried to open her eyes.

'Carrie,' she murmured.

'I thought you'd gone to the angels then, Carrie,' Robert's voice spoke, quite close to her ear, and she opened her eyes at last. He was bending over her. Where they were, she wasn't sure, but it didn't matter. Robert was there, he would take good care of her.

'Oh, Carrie! We were so worried!' That was Judy's voice, and that was Judy's perfume, but by then Carrie had closed her eyes again because her eyelids were so heavy. 'You're to stay in tonight and——'

'Let Nurse West rest now.' *That* was A & E Sister's voice, a soft Irish one.

'Yes, come along, Judy, I'll run you back to your uncle's.' Robert's voice and Judy's perfume both vanished and only A & E Sister's voice remained.

'You had a nasty bump there, Nurse, sure you did, but you'll be all right now. There aren't any bones broken. Some poor old soul was driving along at ten miles an hour when you walked out in front of him! He thought his last hour had come. He'll be glad you're alive,' the buxom sister commented caustically, and Carrie felt like giggling.

'Yes, Sister. No, Sister,' she said instead.

'That will be enough cheek from *you*, my fine lady! Just you rest now and I'll be right back.' The swish of starched skirts was gone and Carrie drifted off to sleep remembering the concern in Robert's voice. He sounded as if he loved her. 'I wonder if he does?' she murmured.

'I wanted you to come and stay with me, Carrie, but Daddy said you couldn't!' That wail came from Ella, and Carrie smiled at her from her uncle's favourite armchair, where she was resting, with Girlie on her lap.

'It wouldn't be right, Ella. It might cause vibrations along the hospital grapevine!' Carrie said teasingly. 'Sarah says she'll come to see you. She was very concerned,' Ella went on, plumping herself down on the rug in front of Carrie. 'She said how awful it would be if you'd had a really bad accident and couldn't walk again!'

'It was kind of her to ask after me,' Carrie said carefully. 'I'm all right, though, really. All I've got to show for it is a skinned knee and two very sore hands!' She held up her hands and Ella pulled a face.

'Ugh! I'm glad I'm not a nurse—or a doctor. I couldn't bear to see people's wounds,' Ella admitted, then Carrie's uncle popped his head around the door.

'Robert's coming to pick up this young lady and I've invited him to supper. Do you think Mrs Cullen will mind?'

If Mrs Cullen minded, Nurse West certainly didn't! 'No, I'm sure she won't.' Mrs Cullen was her uncle's housekeeper, a widow of sixty or so, with a grown-up family and too much time on her hands. Since Aunt Moira's death, she had put in more hours, and Carrie was glad of her company. So was Girlie, the old dog, who waddled patiently after the woman, particularly at mealtimes.

'Oh, what about Judy? She won't be in,' Carrie said, as an afterthought, but her uncle shook his head.

'She was going up to London to sort something out, but she changed her mind.'

Carrie nodded, feeling uneasy. Judy was supposed to be returning to London. Indeed, her agent had rung twice, asking when she would be going back. It wasn't like Judy to leave matters in the air like that. There had to be a good reason for her to stay down here, and Carrie knew exactly what it was: Judy wasn't going home until she had Robert Sheraton's ring on the third finger of her left hand.

'Carrie? You're lost in a brown study, my dear.' Uncle Charles sounded perplexed, and Carrie hastily pulled herself together. What did it matter, anyway? If it wasn't Judy, it would be someone else. What about that woman with the laser eyes? He had soon dropped *her*, so probably Judy's reign wouldn't last long.

'I'm fine, Uncle, really,' she said quickly aware that her uncle was nodding to himself, as if he had found his own solution to the problem. Carrie hoped he was nowhere near the truth!

'Are you coming to the hospital ball, Carrie? Do you good, get you out of yourself a little.' Her uncle raised an enquiring brow, and Carrie found herself agreeing.

'It's a bit starchy, though. I went the first year I

started at St Hilda's. All my set went, for a laugh, but we felt *awful*!'

Uncle Charles smiled. 'It will do you good, and I promise to dance at least once with you. Perhaps I shouldn't be going, but it's in aid of charity, and your aunt would want life to carry on, you know. Do you think she would mind?'

'Oh, Uncle! Of course she wouldn't! I'll dress up, then, and wear the pearls—if you don't mind?' she asked anxiously.

He patted her hand. 'You wear them, Carrie. Moira would be proud of you. Judy must come to the ball as well—two Cinderellas! I'm too old to be Prince Charming but I'll see what I can do about that,' he promised.

Ella looked up from where she was tickling Girlie's tum. 'I wish I could go to the ball,' she said wistfully, and Carrie almost jumped. She'd forgotten Ella.

'Now *you* sound like Cinderella!' Uncle Charles put in, and they were enjoying a therapeutic laugh when Judy let herself in. Carrie glanced up, her eyes full of laughter—to see Judy framed in the doorway, with Robert a pace or two behind, his darkness acting as a perfect foil for Judy's fair beauty. They made a lovely couple, Carrie thought wistfully.

'A variety of expressions crossed your face then, Carrie,' Robert commented, as he greeted his colleague. 'I'm not sure all of them were welcoming. Should I beat a hasty retreat? Or are you not in a consultant-eating mood tonight?'

Carrie wrinkled her nose at him, and Judy laid a hand delicately on his arm. 'You mustn't tease my little sister, Robert! You know how sensitive teenagers are.'

Ella put in pertly, 'Of course he knows that. *I'm* a teenager, but Carrie isn't. She's quite old! I wish *I* was twenty.'

Judy smiled uneasily at Ella. 'I should hate to be twenty again,' she commented, then deftly turned the conversation. At supper, she monopolised Robert to such an extent that no one else bothered to say anything. Carrie thought he might have made some effort to bring the others into the conversation, but, to be fair to him, it was more a monologue than a conversation. Judy never stopped talking and Robert seemed disinclined to add anything other than 'Really?' or 'I'm sure you're right.'

Judy was talking about one of her books now, and Carrie listened more intently, trying to recall which one it was. She had read them all but didn't particularly care for them, since the love interest was usually minimal, and surely that should take centre stage?

'Is that *Search Every Shadow* you're talking about?' she put in, and Judy broke off, looking annoyed.

'Oh, no, this is a new one. I haven't got a title for it yet but it's about—oh, the usual sort of thing,' Judy hurried on.

'It will still be one of those ghastly—or ghostly— horrors, will it?' their uncle asked, and there was a taut silence before Judy shrugged.

'I wouldn't call them that, Uncle Charles. They're very carefully researched.'

Robert had put down his knife and fork and was looking at Judy, a faint smile on his mouth. 'Do you mean you write tales of horror? I thought Carrie said they were romantic sagas?'

'Well, I might have done,' Carrie replied evasively.

'They have romance in them, naturally,' Judy cooed. 'I mean, it's an important part of every novel, isn't it? The hero with eyes for no one but the heroine. Yes, it *is* a romance but there are elements of—well, I suppose you might call my books Gothic romances.'

Carrie would have called them nothing of the sort, and the publisher certainly didn't, but she refrained from saying so. If Judy preferred not to admit to Robert that she wrote gruesome, blood-curdling tales, that was up to her.

'Now,' Judy said brightly, 'I vote that Carrie washes

up and Ella and I shall dry while you men exchange medical chit-chat. Right, Carrie?'

'Of course. Nurses are used to having their hands in water and I——'

'That's lovely!' Judy trilled, getting up and pecking Carrie's cheek. 'You really are a pet! Isn't she, boys?' Without waiting for the 'boys' to respond, she began stacking the plates on the trolley. 'I'm doing my bit, as you can see,' she announced, and Carrie gave a sad smile. Judy's skill at doing her bit usually meant organising other people!

'*I* think Nurse West should be resting,' Robert said gently but firmly, 'so I shall deposit her on the kitchen chair. I think I've seen one in there.' Before Carrie had time to realise what he was doing, Robert had swept her up in his arms and carried her along the narrow passageway to the kitchen at the rear.

Carrie closed her eyes in bliss. This was heaven! Oh, Robert! her heart cried, if only you loved me!

If only I were six years older and glamorous, she told herself as, at last, he set her down upon the far from glamorous kitchen chair that Aunt Moira had always refused to throw away.

'Comfy, Nurse?' Robert's smile was enigmatic, and Carrie nodded, not trusting herself to speak. 'Good. Ella will wash—the gloves are sticking out of that jar, Ella— and I shall wipe while you sit and take things easy. That was a nasty blow you suffered.' He bent and placed a cool hand on Carrie's forehead. 'Sure you're all right now? No headaches or sudden changes of temperature?'

Only when you're near me, Carrie wanted to say. 'No, sir,' she said instead. 'Really, I'm fine.'

In the event, it was Judy who dried the dishes, while Robert and Carrie sat back and watched the proceedings. It took much longer than usual and Carrie's hands itched to get to the washing-up bowl. Ella took her time, washing each article and rinsing it carefully and methodically, while Judy's help consisted mainly of drying one item, then turning to speak to Robert, before reluctantly taking another plate or cup and rubbing it absently while she thought up another topic of conversation. Carrie watched all this with a jaundiced eye, but Robert seemed to be enjoying himself, and several times his husky chuckle warmed her.

Later, Carrie went up to her room, intending to look something out to wear for the hospital ball. Ella padded up behind her and together they went through her meagre wardrobe. As Carrie had once told Robert, Judy was generous and often replenished Carrie's wardrobe as well as her own. Unfortunately, though, her idea of what her little sister could wear wasn't always Carrie's, and many of the clothes found their way to her nursing colleagues. Still, for the ball she could afford to look a bit different. Then there were Aunt Moira's pearls.

'I must show you my pearls, Ella. Aunt Moira left them to me.' Carrie opened the wardrobe, pulled out the drawer, then felt for the hidden catch. 'Here we are——' she began, then stopped. The pearls in their velvet case had gone. 'But they *were* here! Oh, Ella, I've lost them!'

'Perhaps they've been stolen,' Ella suggested. 'A cat burglar,' she went on, clearly excited by the idea.

'We haven't been burgled. No, Judy was right. She said I would lose them and I have. Yet I'm sure I put them back.' Carrie carefully closed the hidden compartment, then the wardrobe, her search for a dress to wear temporarily forgotten. What could she say to Uncle Charles? Aunt Moira should have left them to Judy—*she* wouldn't lose a valuable item like that, not like the scatty Nurse West.

'They'll turn up, I expect. My mother left me a lovely diamond clip and earrings but Daddy won't let me have them yet. I think that's mean of him,' Ella announced. 'Come on, I want to see what you're wearing for the ball.'

Ella dived into the wardrobe and began pulling out

each outfit, clucking over it then putting it back. Evidently nothing was suitable.

Since sitting about wouldn't help, Carrie went through each drawer carefully while Ella was busy. But there was nothing anywhere. The pearls had vanished as if they had never been. How could she confess to Uncle Charles? He would be so hurt.

'Oh, wear this, Carrie!' Ella hauled out a dress Carrie had half thought about giving away. With reddish-brown hair, how could she wear a flame-coloured dress? Another of Judy's kind but misguided ideas.

She shook her head. 'I can't wear that, not with my hair. Anyway, it's much too sophisticated.'

Ella held up the fiery, gauzy dress, her eyes shining. 'I wish I could wear it!'

With your hair and complexion, you would look stunning,' Carrie commented, eyeing the beautiful gown. The colour and material were extravagant, so the dress itself was perfectly plain, with a high round neck and simple, uncluttered lines. She took the dress from Ella, the soft, floaty fabric tempting her. Holding it against her, Carrie took a few turns around the small room, the material floating about her, while Ella uttered exclamations of pleasure.

'Do wear it, Carrie! I'm sure Daddy would like it.'

'Daddy isn't wearing it, *I* am,' Carrie said lightly. 'He would say that a redhead has no business wearing a colour like this. My hair clashes horribly with it.' She wasn't sure whether she was trying to convince Ella or herself.

'You've got lovely hair, Carrie. Daddy said so,' Ella said unexpectedly, just as Carrie's thoughts were turning back to the necklace. 'It's got red and brown and lovely strands of gold running through it. Haven't you noticed? I wish I had red hair.'

'Did Daddy really say so? About my hair, I mean?' Carrie stared at her in astonishment, only half believing her. 'Perhaps I *will* wear this one, so put it back, there's a dear, and I'll have another look for the pearls. It's odd about the case going missing as well. I wonder if——?' Might Judy have borrowed them? No, Judy would have asked first. And had Robert really said she had lovely hair?

That thought kept her going through the rest of the evening.

'Penny for your thoughts, my dear.' Uncle Charles's expression was loving, concerned, and Carrie blushed. If only he knew!

'I was just thinking, that's all,' she said hastily. She thought Robert gave her a considered look but couldn't be sure, for Judy sprang up then and suggested they play Trivial Pursuit. Carrie's heart wasn't in it, and her concerned glance more than once turned upon her uncle.

'Leave him, Carrie.' Robert's voice was quiet, and Carrie started, surprised to be addressed by him since he hadn't said a word to her for what seemed like hours. 'He's better by himself. Judy will make some coffee for us, I think, then Ella and I must be away.' He raised his voice so that her uncle could hear. 'Sorry to tear ourselves away, but I've a conference tomorrow, Charles.'

'Ah, yes, so you have. I'd forgotten,' Uncle Charles murmured. 'On the emotional aspects of gynaecology, isn't it? Yes, you mustn't miss that. I used to like it up there; they always lay on a good spread after the meetings.'

'Up where, Uncle?' Judy asked blankly.

'Birmingham,' Robert answered the question. 'It's a three-day affair. Why don't you join me there?'

To Carrie's immense relief, this question was addressed to her uncle, not to her sister, but it was firmly declined. 'Nothing like your own hearth and home, Robert. *I'll* put the coffee on and Ella can help me. Will you?'

Ella jumped, leaving Carrie and Judy alone with Robert and the sleeping dog.

'You might cheer up, Carrie, you've been looking grim all evening,' Judy said. 'Hasn't she, Robert?'

He nodded. 'I expect you're thinking serious thoughts, aren't you, Carrie?'

'I was wondering what dress to wear for the hospital ball, actually. I thought I might wear Aunt Moira's pearls, too,' Carrie said, wondering if she could lead into the subject gradually.

'Pearls?' Judy said. 'Oh, Aunt Moira's pearls! You can't wear them to some hosital hop, Carrie. You're certain to lose them.' She turned to Robert, smiling up into his face, but it was Robert who said,

'It isn't just a hospital hop, Judy. It's the annual ball. All the consultants, senior nurses will be there. It's just the sort of function where Carrie can wear her pearls. What sort of dress have you got?'

'I haven't made up my mind yet. Anyway, it's going to be a secret!' Carrie announced, reluctant to discuss the red dress in front of Judy.

'I think the devious Nurse West has a gown in mind and she isn't telling us!' Robert chuckled. 'Ah, coffee!' Uncle Charles and Ella appeared with the trolley, and the question of dress—and pearls—was dropped for the time being, though Carrie's mind was fully occupied with the problem.

'May *I* go to the ball as well?' Judy asked, as they were finishing their coffee, and Uncle Charles looked surprised.

'I thought you didn't enjoy "parish pump" functions, Judy! You told me you despised small-town people and small-town——'

'Yes, well, I might have been over-hasty,' Judy put in quickly, and Carrie almost choked. It was just the sort of remark Judy did make, frequently.

'I dare say your uncle will wangle you a ticket,' Robert put in, without, Carrie was relieved to note, offering to take her there himself.

'Carrie's going to wear a beautiful filmy flame dress,'

Ella said, having been out of the room when they were discussing clothes earlier. 'And she was going to wear the pearls but she——' Ella stopped, covering her mouth with her hand, and Carrie just wanted to die. 'Sorry,' Ella muttered. 'I wasn't supposed to say. She's decided not to wear them because I'm going to lend her my crystal beads. Aren't I, Carrie?'

Carrie nodded and murmured something that they might have taken for assent. 'I hope you've put them somewhere safe,' her uncle put in, and Carrie nodded again.

'I put them back where they came from, in the locked drawer at the back of the cupboard. But——' Carrie hesitated, knowing that she must confess. 'I'm sorry, but they aren't there any more, and the case is missing. I must have lost them!' She met her uncle's gaze bravely, but almost flinched at the expression in his eyes.

'Lost them? You've lost Moira's pearls? Already?'

'I'm sure I haven't, Uncle! They aren't lost, just mislaid. I was certain I'd put them back.' Carrie got up and put her arms around her uncle. 'I'll find them. Perhaps I put them away with my toilet things.'

'It didn't take you long to "mislay" them, Carrie!' Judy's voice was cold, accusing, and Carrie turned on her, her eyes stormy.

'That isn't fair! I put them back where they belonged, truly! But——' But where were they now if she did put them back? That was a question she couldn't answer. She became aware that her uncle was patting her arm awkwardly.

'Don't trouble your little head about it now, Carrie. Have a good look later on. I think I'll take a stroll. You might give me a lift to the end of the road, Robert. Then I'll walk back. It will blow the cobwebs away—I'll see if I can prise Girlie away from the fire!'

Robert rose, but Carrie refused to meet his no doubt accusing gaze. She felt such a fool, particularly in front of him. And poor Uncle Charles—what must he be thinking?

'Cheer up, Carrie,' Robert said as she showed them out. 'I'm sure the pearls will turn up. Have a good look around tomorrow, when your brain's fresher. You might remember better then. And take care of yourself—you're precious.'

'A spot of fresh air will do Uncle Charles good,' Carrie said, half to herself, as she surveyed the coffee-cups. Judy wasn't likely to offer to do the dishes now that they were alone, and she felt too tired. 'I'll just stack these in the kitchen for now and go up and have another look for——'

'You won't find them,' Judy broke in awkwardly, and Carrie spun round. 'I borrowed them but I could hardly say so in front of Uncle Charles. He might not like my taking them.'

'I don't like your taking them, either,' Carrie said. 'Why on earth couldn't you ask me? And why didn't you own up when I said they were missing? Now Uncle Charles will think I've lost them!'

'Not if they're back in their hidey-hole by the time he gets back,' Judy pointed out. 'I borrowed them for a special date and I forgot to put them back, if you must know. I *was* going to ask you but you went off and got yourself run over and there wasn't time.'

'I'm sorry about that.'

Judy appeared not to notice the sarcasm in Carrie's tone, for she hurried on, 'It can't be helped now. I've got them in my case. I'll put them in one of your drawers, shall I? Then you can honestly say you've found them, can't you?'

'Yes, I could, I suppose. *What* special date?' Carrie asked, and Judy shrugged.

'Oh, someone took me wining and dining, and I wanted to look good. I really am awfully sorry, pet. I know I shouldn't have borrowed them, but they *do* suit me.'

Judy looked so contrite, so honestly sorry, that Carrie couldn't sustain her anger. What did it matter, anyway? The pearls were safe, that was all that mattered. She hugged her sister, and Judy dropped a kiss on her brow. 'There, that's for my kid sister and her understanding. You're growing up, kid sister. You aren't a child any more,' Judy went on slowly.

Carrie smiled. 'I'm glad you've noticed. Before long, I'll be a staff nurse, then a ward sister. I might end up running the hospital!'

Judy chuckled. 'I can't quite see that happening; you'll be married and having babies long before that, but——' She hesitated, glancing down at her scarlet fingernails. 'Look, pet, you aren't falling for Robert Sheraton, are you? Because if you are, I can tell you it isn't a bit of use. He——'

'Of course I'm not!' Perhaps Carrie denied it too vehemently, for Judy didn't look convinced.

'That's just as well, because he's spoken for, I can assure you of that! You're young, and, well, easily hurt, vulnerable, and I don't want Robert to hurt you. Leave him alone, he's too much man for you. Why don't you concentrate on that young student we saw you with? He's more your age and——'

'You mean the one I was grappling with the evening I was knocked down?' Carrie's face was grim. 'No, thank you, and yes, I *did* know Robert was spoken for. He's way out of my league, as you say. Will you put the pearls away? Uncle Charles will be back soon. It isn't far to walk from the corner of the road.'

'Yes, all right, but remember what I said. You have an unfortunate habit of falling for medics, you know. Look what happened to Hal,' Judy said, her long legs already carrying her to the stairs before Carrie could recover.

'Yes, look what happened to Hal—*you* stole him,' Carrie said softly, but Judy didn't hear.

CHAPTER THIRTEEN

'IF YOU answer the exam questions as well as you have that one, I see no reason why you shouldn't pass with flying colours,' Robert Sheraton commented as Carrie finished explaining about the emotional aspects of gynaecological surgery.

Then he got up and stretched, yawning, and Carrie hastily looked away. She didn't want to look at him, she didn't! And she certainly didn't want him as a brother-in-law. Yet Judy had confessed on the telephone only the previous evening that she was thinking of settling down. That meant only one thing: Robert must be on the brink of proposing. Or Judy thought she could bring him to the brink, which might not be the same thing. Judy might find Robert harder to handle than she thought! He wasn't a man to fall for a woman's wiles just like that.

'Nurse West?'

Aware that Robert was waiting for a reply, and must, therefore, have asked her a question, Carrie hastily rose, smoothing down her apron. They were in the ward office of Men's Medical, Willow Ward, and she had been on the way to give a patient an injection when the sister had told her the consultant gynaecologist wanted to see her in the office.

'Sorry, sir. Did you ask me something?'

Dark eyes gazed thoughtfully at her, then Robert shook his head. 'It doesn't matter. It—wasn't that important.' He ran his fingers through his thick dark hair, leaving it rumpled as though he had just woken from sleep, and Carrie felt desire rise within her. But Judy was right; he was too much man for her. She ought to stick to boys of her own age. Damn Judy! she thought suddenly, feeling an almost physical pain.

'Thank you for putting me through my paces, Mr Sheraton.' Carrie spoke clearly, as much for the benefit of the ward sister who was hovering in the corridor as for the surgeon himself. The fact that 'Caroline's Conquest' had taken the trouble to seek her out at the opposite end of the hospital would cause a great deal of comment, but at least Robert had a good reason.

'Just take your time, answer each question to the best of your ability, and don't worry about the questions you can't answer very well. Even the best nurse can't know everything.' Robert's smile was warm, and Carrie had to make a conscious effort not to smile back.

'Thank you, sir, I appreciate it. And so does Uncle Charles, I mean Dr Warriner,' she hurried on. 'I hope I don't let you both down.'

'I hope so, too, Nurse. Have you any final questions?' Robert glanced at his watch, evidently keen to get back to his clinic. 'Oh—by the way,' he went on, before Carrie could begin the apology she simply *must* deliver, 'have you given any thought to your own feelings? How would *you* feel if you were told you faced a serious gynae operation? Describe your feelings, Nurse West.' Robert sat down again, a little smile lurking around his eyes.

Carrie hesitated, then plunged on, 'I would feel less of a woman, I think. If the operation were hysterectomy,' she amended. 'And I—I would feel a has-been, of no use any more, I suppose,' she went on thoughtfully. Of course she always tried to put herself in the patient's place, the emotions that were passing through the patient's mind, but at twenty it wasn't always possible to imagine how a woman would feel at the menopause, or on being told she had to have her womb removed and could have no more children. At such times, Carrie knew women often felt as though their whole world had ended, and she tried to express this to Robert, who, despite being a man, obviously *did* understand a woman's feelings at such time, and was as concerned about the psychological aspects of surgery as he was about the operation itself.

'I would be depressed, too,' she added, and Robert nodded encouragingly.

'Why?' he probed.

'The ending of an era?' Carrie suggested. 'Perhaps no more children, or the fear of malignancy. Loss of femininity—I wouldn't feel *whole* any more.'

'Quite right. And if a pregnancy is terminated, then guilt feelings are usually strong as well. Sometimes marriages break down after a gynae operation, or a severe strain is placed upon the relationship. Bear all these points in mind, Nurse, and you will sail through. And be a better nurse,' Robert added. 'Exams are all very well, but they aren't an end in themselves.'

Carrie nodded happily, then her face clouded. She owed the man an apology yet again, and she might as well get it over with. She would far rather have spent another hour talking about disturbances of the female reproductive system, but this couldn't wait any longer.

'I have to apologise, sir!' she burst out. 'About Mrs Jordan and—and her flat. You *do* care about working people and I shouldn't have said you didn't!'

'Ah, yes, Mrs Jordan.' Robert's voice was soft, but there was no mistaking the menacing expression in his eyes, and Carrie braced herself for a verbal beating. Well, it was no more than she deserved, but hadn't she prompted him to do a good deed? Quite by chance, she had found out that the comfortable and spacious flat Eileen Jordan and her husband were living in now had been provided by the consultant gynaecologist himself! Apparently, he owned the house and had decided to convert it into flats, to be let out cheaply to those in need.

'You remember,' she prompted, 'in the corridor, when you were with Judy, I told you off and——'

'I seem to remember several occasions when you have

"told me off", as you put it,' he said, still speaking quietly, and Carrie was unable to deny that.

'I think it's made you more human,' she said tactlessly, then rushed on just as an obviously astonished surgeon began to speak, 'No, please let me finish. I know I ought not to speak to a consultant like this and—and you can have me thrown out. Well, perhaps not, but I've been in trouble before for speaking my mind and——'

Robert held up a hand, and Carrie ground to a halt. There was so much she wanted to say to him and her poor tongue couldn't get around all the words. She could put a sentence together with the best of them, but, when she was faced with velvety dark eyes, a sexy mouth and the dear, dear face of the man she loved, good English grammar went out of the hospital window!

'I accept your apology, tactlessly worded though it was, Nurse West. And I'm delighted to know that I have become more human, less concerned with a life of idleness and debauchery. Now, I really must go. Good luck with the Croxton Prize.'

'Oh, but I wanted——' But he was gone and Carrie was left staring at the closed door. She hadn't meant that, of course she hadn't. There was nothing idle *or* debauched about Robert.

She was still staring into space when the Willow Ward sister strode briskly in. 'All finished, Nurse? Good. You were lucky to have a consultant gynae put you through your paces for the Croxton. Still, it comes of being related to another consultant, doesn't it? They stick together. Now, if you're back with us, I want you to help Staff. The bedpans and bottles have gone round. Heaven help anyone who wants one now!'

Carrie had opened her mouth to protest that it was nothing to do with her uncle's being a consultant, then thought better of it. If Sister thought that, other people might, too. It was better than the question of 'Caroline's Conquest' being recalled to mind!

The Croxton Prize was awarded to nurses who were,

like Carrie, in their second year of training, and it was greatly coveted. The names of previous winners were displayed in the main entrance of the hospital itself. The students had to answer every question on the paper, which was a long one, and would be good practice for the finals.

Carrie knew she wouldn't win the prize, but she was determined not to let the school or her uncle down if she could help it. Every question must be tackled as though it were on the finals paper, hence Uncle Charles asking Robert if he would put some searching questions to her when he had a minute. If she hoped Robert would call at the house and she could be alone with him, she was to be disappointed. It seemed to her that he had deliberately chosen the most public place possible. It was as if he didn't want to be alone with her, and Carrie knew she must have hurt his feelings dreadfully.

Then, too, he was probably thinking she was a silly, feckless girl for losing the valuable pearls, for she hadn't told anyone about Judy. Uncle Charles had been delighted when the pearls were produced, and hadn't asked any searching questions. It might be best not to wear them for the ball, which was due to be held after the Croxton tests. Carrie smiled to herself. It was something exciting to look forward to, and she was determined that she would enjoy herself, Robert Sheraton or no Robert Sheraton!

There were thirty-four patients in Willow Ward, and it was difficult to remember all their names. Carrie wasn't one of those nurses who called patients 'Grandad' or 'dear'. She liked to address them by name, but it was proving hard going, particularly as the two auxiliaries thought she needn't bother.

'I just call them "love"', one said as she helped Carrie sit up old Mr Wathen later. 'They don't mind and it saves trying to remember who they are!' She chuckled, but Carrie didn't think it was funny.

'I have to help with the medicine round so I *need* to

know their names. And I have to keep up with their
medical conditions, know about taking tests, and so on,'
she pointed out. 'I don't think calling people "love"
matters. I expect they like it, but I would never remember their names at all if I did that,' she rushed on, aware
that her runaway tongue might cause offence. In a ward
like Willow, there were more nursing aides than trained
staff, and by and large they were good workers, kind to
the patients, and much loved by them. It wouldn't do to
upset them, but Carrie couldn't help longing for the
discipline of gynae. How Sister Carter would laugh if she
knew!

'That's true, dear,' the auxiliary said complacently. 'Is
that better, love?' This remark was addressed to Mr
Wathen, a man of nearly eighty-nine, who had poor lung
function and suffered frequent bouts of bronchitis. He
was a candidate for the geriatric wing, but he was
mentally alert and lived alone when he wasn't on one of
his frequent admissions, and Carrie had grown to like
him.

'You're a lovely girl, Mildred,' Mr Wathen wheezed,
and Carrie pouted.

'What about me?' Aren't I lovely, too, Mr Wathen?'

'Course you are, dear. I bin saying to old Fred over
there. . .' Mr Wathen indicated his bed neighbour
'. . . I said she's got a lovely sunny smile, that little girl.
I'll bet she has all the boys after her!'

'I wish I had,' Carrie said lightly, flushed with
pleasure. At least she was a hit with *somebody*!

Carrie stored up tales about the patients ready for her
regular visits to Ann Haynes, now Ann Mackie. Ann
had astonished everyone, including Carrie, by disconin-
uing her training and bringing forward her marriage to
Phil Mackie. She now worked part-time as a doctors'
receptionist, but only Carrie knew the real reason for the
change—Ann had thought she was pregnant. That had
now been confirmed, and, to Carrie's surprise, her
tearful friend had turned into an almost calm pregnant

lady. Now Ann had a status; she wasn't just a rather mediocre student nurse, she was a *doctor's* wife.

It was Ann who mentioned Eileen Jordan. 'Wasn't it great of Mr Sheraton to find Eileen a flat?' she enthused. 'Did you hear about it, Carrie?'

'Yes, on the grapevine! I was surprised, though. I mean, he more or less said there wasn't anything he could do for her social problems.' Carrie didn't intend mentioning her part in his change of heart. 'Did he say why he changed his mind?'

'He didn't change his mind, Carrie! It's an ongoing project, he told me all about it.'

'He did? When?' Carrie leaned forward.

'Oh, a week or so ago. He'll be delivering the baby, you know. He's taking an interest. Here.' Ann reached over for a workbox. 'He bought us this. Isn't it sweet?'

A large soft teddy bear gazed at Carrie out of sensuous dark eyes, and she nearly choked. 'Oh, it's lovely, Ann! I never thought. . .' Her voice trailed away.

'No, you never thought much of him at first, did you? You were always tearing strips off him just because he was rich. But he does care.' Ann sat back, a little smile on her face. 'You love him, don't you? I always thought it was sour grapes on your part because he preferred Sister Carter.'

'No!' Carrie almost jumped up in indignation. Ann's remark was far too accurate. 'I—I *like* him. Now,' she amended, trying to be fair. 'But he has changed. Even you have to admit that.'

'Ye-es, I suppose so. Perhaps he's in love,' Ann said.

'He is. With my sister, I think. You've met Judy, haven't you?'

Ann giggled. 'Fancy her and old Sheraton! Who would have thought it!'

'He isn't old!' Carrie flashed, then wished she had kept her mouth shut as Ann smiled triumphantly.

'I knew it! You do fancy him! Still, once you're qualified you'll be more on his level. He can't have a torrid affair with a student nurse, can he? It wouldn't be good for his career—or yours.' She hesitated, before rushing on, 'He's probably better with Judy, you know. I don't suppose *she* tells him he doesn't care enough about the poor people of this world! He and his aunt something-or-other, they've got this project. There's some trust fund and it's to benefit local people. Eileen Jordan's local, born and bred here, or so she told me once. The trust owns houses and flats which they rent out cheaply. Though if it hadn't been for you I don't suppose Mr Sheraton would have realised her plight, so you weren't entirely mistaken about him.'

No, not entirely, but that didn't make it any easier to bear. She had treated him abominably and he hadn't attempted to defend himself. She had called him, what was it? Too rich to care. Something like that, anyway. Whatever it was, Carrie knew she had wasted her chances, if she had ever *had* a chance with Robert Sheraton.

Carrie was hardly surprised when Judy decided to stay in Gainsborough a little longer. The trips she made to London were brief, and most nights she spent at their uncle's home, Carrie herself having gone back to the nurses' home. Uncle Charles seemed to be coping well, and he did, after all, have an absorbing job to keep him occupied. In the evenings, there was Judy's bright conversation, unless she went out.

'There are less distractions down here, Carrie, love,' Judy almost purred a few days later. 'When is this wonderful ball, though? I mustn't miss that!'

'Saturday week,' Carrie said quietly. 'It's the day after the Croxton exams.' That landmark loomed large in her life at present, though it didn't push Robert out of her mind, unfortunately.

'Ugh! You students and your exams! What are you going to wear for the ball? Oh, and will you be wanting the pearls? I don't think they're really suitable for a young——' Judy stopped, warned by Carrie's mutinous face.

'Of course you can borrow them. I'm sure Uncle Charles won't mind,' Carrie said evenly. 'I'm wearing that pretty flame-coloured dress you bought me last year.'

'Oh, lovely! You'll be a wow, Carrie!' Judy assured her. 'And don't worry about wearing red, either. It's super for redheads, all the rage.'

Whether Robert Sheraton would think so was another question, since he had asked Judy to accompany him to the ball.

'I thought he wasn't going to ask, you know,' Judy confessed. 'He's taken his time. It would serve him right if someone else asked me, wouldn't it? I can tease him about being a lucky man that I'm free!'

'You can't do that to him,' Carrie protested. 'He'll be terribly hurt. Oh, Judy, you wouldn't!'

'Why should it matter to you?' Judy wanted to know, then she nodded to herself. 'I see. I told you not to get involved, didn't I? He's a consultant, for heaven's sake! They're supposed to be little gods, aren't they? Just think what the hospital would say if he announced that he was shacking up with a junior nurse!'

'It wouldn't be "shacking up", as you call it. I love him! But I know there isn't any future in it, and you needn't be afraid I'll try to steal him from you—I'm not that stupid!'

Judy made no further comment, but Carrie didn't like her expression. It was worried, puzzled and exasperated all in one.

Robert's voice on the telephone that evening completely threw her. Her uncle had picked her up from St Hilda's after her late duty and she was just beginning a couple of days off, days she had decided to spend with Uncle Charles and Judy. Now she held the receiver a little away from her, wondering and worrying—had Judy said anything?

'Carrie? Are you still there?' Robert sounded faintly amused.

'Yes, I'm still here. And I'd love to spend Saturday with Ella—if I can get someone to swap with me. I've had my days off. Will she come here? I've got something to show her.'

There was a pause. 'No, I think you had better come here. Ella wants to take you on a guided tour of my aunt's house. You couldn't stay for that last time, could you? Judy has the advantage of you there. She must have poked into every nook and cranny when she was here.'

'I'm not going to do that!' Carrie protested. 'Anyway, what I wanted to show Ella is a kitten. Well, it's almost a cat, really. It's a stray and I——'

'And kind Nurse West took pity on it. Oh, Carrie!'

'It followed me! I found it behind the nurses' home, scavenging, and I couldn't bear the look in its eyes,' she confessed, without any real expectation that Robert would understand.

'You're a sweet soul, Carrie, and that kitten has taken unfair advantage of you. I expect someone told it Nurse West took in waifs and strays!'

Robert was laughing at her! She could hear him trying to control his mirth.

'Anyway,' he went on after a moment, his voice muffled, 'Bert—that's Aunt Aggie's odd-job man and chauffeur—will pick you up about coffee-time on Saturday. I must go now, I've a friend coming.'

Since Judy was also engaged for the evening, it didn't take much intelligence to work out who Robert's friend might be.

On Saturday, it wasn't Bert who turned up bright and early, long before Carrie was ready, it was Robert Sheraton himself. Judy was still in the bathroom, and Carrie was just washing up after breakfast, her old flowered housecoat barely covering her. The last thing she wanted was a visitor, and she was tempted not to answer the doorbell. She was lucky to get the day off when she had already had two days, and she was afraid it might be a colleague telling her she had to work after all!

Still. . . Sighing, and trying to hover behind the door, Carrie inched it open—to meet the enigmatic smile of the last person she expected to see. 'Oh! It's you,' she said blankly.

'Yes, I think it's me. Am I unwelcome? Or too early, perhaps?' The smile had vanished, and Carrie's heart sank. He knew she loved him! Judy must have told him.

'Too early, we aren't up yet—oh, and Judy wanted to come as well and——'

'She can't,' he said bluntly. 'Am I to be kept on the doorstep, or will you allow me in while you get ready? I'm not going to steal the family silver—or that pearl necklace,' he went on grimly, and Carrie very nearly closed the door in his face.

'You've no right to remind me about that!' She took the chain off the door reluctantly, then hurried through to her uncle's study, leaving the consultant to close the front door. She had to find something else to put on; she mustn't let Robert see her like this! She had forgotten that he would have an excellent view of her bare legs before she finally disappeared into the study. This led through to the conservatory, and Carrie made her way upstairs by this devious route, returning a few minutes later in jeans and sweatshirt, her face flushed. 'Sorry about that, but I wasn't dressed for visitors,' she explained. 'Would you like some coffee?'

Robert surveyed her through half-closed lashes. 'Why not? You're looking very young today,' he added, indicating the luxuriant hair which Carrie hadn't bothered to tie back. She wasn't wearing make-up, either, though she had been tempted to dab on a little lipstick, before deciding against it. 'I'm sorry Ella couldn't come with me,' he went on, 'but she was out riding and I slipped away early. I needed time to think.'

What he needed to think about, he didn't say and

Carrie thought it better not to ask. In silence, she poured him a coffee, then sat at the table while he drank it, her head bent, her own mind busy as well.

'Thank you, that was just what I needed,' he said at last, and, still without speaking, Carrie took his cup over to the sink.

'I took Judy out to dinner on Thursday,' he spoke into the lengthening silence.

'Oh, did you? She said she had a dinner date, but she didn't say who with,' Carrie said, with a calmness she didn't feel. Was he about to tell her he and Judy were engaged? No, Judy would have said something. No way could she have kept such exciting news to herself.

'She was wearing pearls—your pearls, presumably. Did she ask permission this time? Or last time?' he probed, and Carrie swung round in astonishment.

Before she could speak, Robert continued, 'No, I can see she didn't. Why didn't you tell Charles she borrowed them before? Why take the blame for losing them?'

Before Carrie could collect her scattered wits, think up some excuse, Robert moved closer, and she caught her breath. Oh, please don't let him touch me! she said silently. She was sure to give herself away if he did.

'Carrie——' he began seriously, and she wondered what was coming. Then a movement behind him caught her eye, and she broke into a relieved smile.

'This is Felix, sir. Say hello to the nice surgeon, Felix.' She held out her hand, and Robert turned around, to see the stray half-grown cat slink into the room.

'Good morning, Felix,' he said gravely, and the cat paused as if unsure of his welcome. Then, completely ignoring Robert, he went over to Carrie and rubbed himself against her legs.

'There you are! He loves me already,' she said proudly. 'Perhaps men have ill-treated him in the past. You don't suppose. . .?' Carrie hesitated, the more so since Robert's expression was anything but encouraging. 'Ella couldn't have Felix, I suppose? Does she like cats?'

'Yes, to both questions, Carrie. I realise you can't have him at the nurses' home and you can hardly leave him for Charles to look after. Yes, we'll take him back with us. I imagine the dog will be glad to get rid of him!'

Carrie nodded. 'Girlie doesn't see very well, and she's completely ignored Felix! She isn't quite sure what he is and why he's in the house, I think. I'm sure Ella would love him! I expect he's good at catching things.'

'Birds, most probably, one of the cat's less pleasant habits,' Robert said drily. 'But I suppose we can try him.' He hesitated, then took a turn about the kitchen, peering out of the big window which overlooked the rambling garden, then pausing by the sink to stare at the washing-up.

'If there's something you want to say to me, sir, shall we get it over with, then I can finish the dishes and nip upstairs to get ready?' Carrie said unsteadily.

'Yes,' he agreed. 'You have a lovely nature, Carrie. Make sure people don't take advantage of you.'

'No one has, as far as I know. Well, Judy might sometimes,' Carrie conceded, 'but she's my sister and I love her. She helped to bring me up. And it didn't really matter about the pearls. They were safe, that was what mattered.'

Robert didn't appear to be attending to her, for he had gone back to staring out at the garden, and all Carrie's fears returned. He *was* going to tell her he loved Judy! No, it was better not to know. She wouldn't give him the opportunity to say anything.

'I'll just pop up and change,' she said brightly. 'Perhaps you could make friends with Felix. Shan't be a minute.' She was out of the kitchen before Robert could call her back, and it was a perplexed Carrie who threw off the jeans and shirt, then hesitated before hammering on the bathroom door. She would just have to disturb Judy. It wouldn't be possible to keep Robert's presence in the house a secret, as she had wished.

'Robert? He's here? Why didn't you tell me?' Judy

flung the words at her as she rushed out of the bathroom, a cloud of perfume following her lightly clad figure. Carrie watched, wide-eyed, as Judy paused on the landing, took a deep breath, then walked sedately down the stairs. She had hardly anything on! Surely she wasn't going to talk to Robert like *that*?

She was, for Carrie heard Judy greet him. She didn't stay to hear any more, her heart heavy.

For once, Carrie had chosen her outfit carefully, and ironically it was one that Judy had bought for her out of the proceeds of *The Evil Eye*. A swirly skirt of off-white with navy edging to the pleats was teamed with a plain jacket, and Carrie wore her favourite blouse with it, a pin-tucked chiffon in a rich emerald, perfect with her hair. At the back of her mind was the thought that she ought to buy a new gown for the ball, something in blue, perhaps. The flame-coloured dress was adventurous, but would Robert like it. . .?

Carrie ventured down to the sitting-room. They were there, with the door half closed, and she hesitated. Ought she to. . .? Yes! Why shouldn't she? Robert had come to see her, not Judy! But had he? a little voice asked her, then sniggered as if it knew the answer. Well, so did she, but it made no difference. She was going to disturb them, anyway.

'Sorry to keep you,' she said breathlessly, as she posed in the doorway in the way she had often seen Judy do.

'Come in, Carrie, do! There's a draught with the door open,' Judy complained. 'If you've quite finished with the bathroom, I'll go back. See you, Robert!' Without a backward glance, Judy was gone, her perfume lingering in the room like a silent and unseen presence.

Robert looked grim-faced, and Carrie wondered whether they had quarrelled. 'Will Judy be long? Have I got time to find Felix? I expect he's disappeared.' Felix didn't like Judy, for some reason.

'Judy isn't coming,' Robert said harshly. 'My invitation was to you, Carrie, not your sister. Or Felix, for that matter, but we'll take him with us. I'll be in the car.'

Robert strode out of the room, leaving a perplexed Carrie to seek out the cat. Then she went in search of Robert, who silently opened the rear door for her and Felix, and just as silently started the engine. It wasn't until they were out of sight of the house that he seemed to relax, and began a conversation, but Carrie made sure she didn't touch on anything personal. They spoke about the hospital, considered whether Felix might settle down, and what to do with him if he didn't. It wasn't until they reached the subject of the St Hilda's ball that Carrie tensed.

'Have you decided what to wear, Carrie?' he asked, as they neared the end of their journey.

'It's filmy and bright red,' she said soberly. 'Well, flame-coloured, plain with a round neck, but I may wear something else.' She waited, but to her disappointment he made no comment.

'Here we are.' Robert's voice broke into her sombre thoughts. 'It's a pity about Felix; we'll have to restrain him or he'll be off to the woods.'

'What woods? I——Oh!'

'I cheated. This is *my* home, not Aunt Aggie's. I thought you would like to see how rich consultants live.' He gave her his slow smile, but Carrie turned away, still clutching Felix. She didn't want to know how he lived; it would be too painful.

The house was much smaller than his aunt Aggie's, and she saw now that they were at the back of Cross Street. The house was one she had admired in the past, only modest-sized, but the garden was huge and rather wild, with apple trees in the front next to shrubs Carrie had never seen before. Along the side of the house Carrie could see more fruit trees and bushes, and a section of kitchen garden. The garden itself backed on to a small area of woodland.

'No flunkies, I'm afraid, but I have a housekeeper.

She and her husband look after the place for me, though I tend to spend a lot of time with my aunt.'

Once inside the door, they set a wide-eyed Felix down, and he and the housekeeper eyed one another. 'He'll want a box, really. Is he paper-trained?' Mrs Murdoch asked, and Carrie nodded.

'Just about. We've had one or two accidents but I think that's because he likes to wee by himself. He hates being watched.'

'Understandable,' Robert murmured, and Carrie joined in the laughter.

'Really, Mr Sheraton, the things you say! Come along, Felix, and I'll give you a wee bite.' Mrs Murdoch bustled away, followed after a pause by the cat.

'Give yourself an unguided tour of the house, Carrie. I've one or two papers to see to in my study, then we'll get along,' Robert suggested, and Carrie needed no second telling.

It was a fairly modern, mock-Georgian house, only two-storey, but the rooms were large and square, and so spacious that she sighed, thinking of her cell-like room in the nurses' home.

She decided to begin upstairs and work her way down to the kitchen. She hesitated in the doorway of what was obviously Robert's own room. The door was wide open so she didn't need to go in. Yes, there was his old-fashioned brush set on the big antique dressing-table. A massive wardrobe stood against one wall, with a tallboy on which stood a bowl and pitcher, to Carrie's delight.

The colour scheme was masculine yet light, with primrose-patterned wallpaper, and touches of white and brown, echoed in the bedspread which covered the double bed.

There were two further bedrooms on that floor, neither of which appeared to be in use. The beds were stripped, the rooms holding an unoccupied air, though in the smaller of the bedrooms there was a giant poster on the wall depicting one of the more popular groups, so evidently Ella used that room for weekends when she wasn't with her great-aunt. Ella had told her she was a weekly boarder at school.

A huge bathroom complete with modern circular bath and a shower cabinet, was the only other room on that floor, but an extending ladder led to a loft space and, after a moment's hesitation, Carrie climbed up, to find what was obviously Ella's 'den'. There were books everywhere, articles of sports gear, a compact disc player, with CDs lying around untidily. But what caught Carrie's eye was the photograph, in a silver frame, which stood on top of a minute desk in one corner of the little room.

She didn't touch it, didn't need to pick it up. There, staring out at her, was a picture of Mireille Sheraton, Ella's mother. The likeness to Ella was remarkable, the soft doe eyes, the rich black hair, the snub nose, that casual air of elegance which would be Ella's greatest asset once she was an adult.

This, then, was the woman Robert had loved and lost, the woman who had died on the operating table. Perhaps she was the only woman he would ever love.

Carrie retraced her steps, wondering at first why the photograph wasn't in Robert's own room. Then she realised—it was too painful for him. Probably he had other photographs of his wife hidden away, taken out and gazed at whenever he was in a sad mood. Feeling sad herself, Carrie went in search of him. The study door was open and he glanced up as she stood there.

'Finished the tour of inspection? It's what the estate agents call a "des res"! Do you approve of it, or do you think I should convert it into flats for the needy? Or bed-sits for drop-outs, perhaps?'

Carrie closed the door firmly before advancing into the room. 'Robert, please don't! You make me feel guilty. I'm sorry I said you didn't care about the needy. You do, and please stop teasing me!' she flashed, seeing the gleam of amusement in his eyes. That was all she was good for, a cheap laugh!

'I'm sorry, too, my poor child. I had no right——'

'Will you stop calling me a child?' Carrie exploded, surprising herself as well as the consultant. 'I'm not a child—I'm as capable of falling in love as an older woman!'

Carrie stopped, horrified by her outburst. Now she had told him everything. And there was still Mireille's photograph upstairs, mocking her foolish love.

'What I mean is, I'm not——' she began.

But she wasn't allowed to say what she meant, for Robert took her in his arms and began kissing her so thoroughly that all coherent thought left her.

CHAPTER FOURTEEN

AFTER a long moment, Robert's lips left Carrie's and began a slow, sensuous trail down her face, her ears, her throat, before returning and kissing the corner of her mouth. This was nothing like the kisses she had endured from Phil. Oh, she had enjoyed them at the time, thought him a practised lover. Hadn't she been tempted, once, to given in to his demands that they consummate their love? She realised now that Phil had a lot to learn, that he was a mere beginner compared with this man. Even Hal, whom she had thought she loved and would always love, hadn't kissed her like this. She snuggled closer to him, fitting her body against his, demanding more, all her good intentions flying out into the spring day. She would make him forget Mireille, forget Judy and all the others, she would, she would!

Robert's mouth was forcing open her lips, his tongue moving around inside, driving her crazy. Her legs felt like jelly. Sometimes in novels she had read about that happening, but had never quite believed it. But it was true!

Then his kisses became more demanding, less gentle, and Carrie felt he was driving the breath from her body. She was afire from the top of her head down to the tips of her toes, the room was spinning, spinning. . .

When they broke apart, Carrie couldn't speak for a moment. She was breathless, with a frightening ache in her heart. If only he loved her!

Robert was breathing harshly, and he moved away from her for a moment. Carrie leaned against the back of the settee, her thoughts in turmoil, her body cold now, chilled. Then she heard his voice, deep and intense with desire.

'That wasn't love, Carrie, that was lust. Is that what you want? A passionate affair?' The words were torn from him, and Carrie put out her hands, eager to offer comfort.

Then she dropped them again, because she saw the face of a stranger, a stranger with Robert's eyes, his features, his athletic body, but a stranger nevertheless. Even his eyes were darker, anguished, almost despairing, she fancied. And it was her fault, she had brought this upon them both. But she was glad!

'I wouldn't mind an affair, if that's what you want,' she heard herself saying. One part of her mind stood off, horrified by her remark, the other half silently applauded. Now at last he knew, if he had ever been in doubt.

'"I wouldn't mind an affair",' he repeated, shaking his head dazedly. 'Hardly a passionate way of putting it.' He smiled grimly. 'Oh, Carrie! If only you knew! We'd better sample some of Mrs Murdoch's home baking, then we'll be away. Shall we leave Felix here?'

Gone was the passionate man in whose arms she had found heaven—or hell. In his place was the consultant surgeon, father of a daughter not that much younger than Carrie herself. She nodded, too full to speak, and he stood aside to let her precede him to the kitchen.

She thought Mrs Murdoch glanced at them appraisingly but the housekeeper made no comment, beyond indicating the cat. 'He'll settle down, if you give him time. We all need time,' she added.

'Yes, that's true. Ella will be keen to get back to see him!' She forced lightness into her voice, so did Robert. He even cracked a joke with his housekeeper. But they were both glad to get away, even though they would be sitting side by side on the journey to his aunt's house. This time there would be no Felix to provide a diversion.

They were nearly at his aunt's mansion before Robert spoke, and Carrie tensed herself. Surely, *now*, he wouldn't mention Judy? 'I'd like to say I'm sorry about what happened, Carrie, my pet, but I won't. I'm not sorry; it had to happen.' He paused, while Carrie's heart sank lower and lower. 'As far as I'm concerned,' he went on, as though nothing important, earth-shattering, had happened between them, 'nothing has changed. You're still a junior nurse and I'm still a consultant. I ought to feel ashamed of myself, but I can't say I am.' He laughed shortly, and Carrie waited, not wanting to break the spell. 'I enjoyed our embrace. It won't happen again, though. Just keep out of my way and don't tempt me, Carrie. I'm only a man with a man's weaknesses, not some plaster saint, for God's sake!'

'No,' she agreed quietly.

'Sarah—Sarah Nugent—she will probably be there. She——'

'There's no need to explain. It's obvious she cares for you,' Carrie said stolidly. 'But so does Judy!'

'Judy? I doubt that Judy cares for anyone except Judy.' Robert's tone was bitter, and Carrie let the matter drop. At least it meant he wasn't about to announce his engagement to her sister! But there was still Sarah Nugent, a woman Carrie couldn't fight. Sarah deserved some happiness. Carrie sighed. Life was becoming very complicated.

Thankfully, Sarah Nugent wasn't there, and Carrie's heart lightened. Nor was Aunt Aggie, who was, in Ella's words 'Doing her good deeds'.

As promised, Ella gave her a guided tour of the old house, which was much bigger and grander than the consultant's, yet Carrie preferred his; it was cosy, had a happy atmosphere.

Appledore. Even the name suggested long summer days, a happy family gathering apples or raiding the soft fruit bushes, laughing and talking, spreading their happiness around. . . A soft smile lit Carrie's face, and Ella had to speak twice before she reluctantly left her dream. A real home and a real family—Robert's home and

Robert's family. Two boys and a second daughter for him.

'Carrie! Do come along! We'll be late for lunch if we don't hurry and Cook doesn't like it if her meals spoil. Aunt Aggie should be back by then. What were you thinking about?'

Carrie shook her head, the foxy hair flying in all directions, for she had left it down. 'I can't tell you, it's a secret. Don't you ever daydream, wish for——? Oh, I don't know. Make secret wishes?'

Ella nodded emphatically. 'Yes, I wish I had a mother. Daddy hardly ever speaks about my real mother. Oh, if I ask him, he'll talk about her, but not otherwise. It's—it's as if she never existed,' the child went on thoughtfully, and Carrie put out a hand and stroked her hair.

'I feel the same way sometimes,' she confessed. 'We're both poor little orphans!'

Carrie learned more about Mireille from Robert's aunt, when she went to say goodbye to her that evening. 'You see, Carrie, my dear, Robert has loved only once, but he loved not wisely but too well,' Aunt Aggie explained, her eyes soft as they rested upon Carrie. 'He adored Mireille, there's no doubt of that, and she, I suppose, loved him in her own way. They were a handsome, glamorous couple, but not right for each other, you know. Now he can't love again; he's too wary, too—unsure of himself, perhaps.'

There was nothing unsure about Robert Sheraton, but Carrie didn't like to say so. 'Perhaps he hasn't met the right woman,' she murmured, and the old lady gave her a strange look.

'Perhaps. Or perhaps he has found someone to love but the obstacles are too great. This woman may be married, or from a——'

'Or too young, only a junior nurse,' Carrie said quietly, and the old lady sighed.

'Yes, she could be a junior nurse. With Robert having a teenage daughter—well, you can see the difficulties, can't you? Or maybe you can't. When we are young, we tend to see only what we want to see. If you are to succeed with my nephew, you will have to make him see that age doesn't matter, it's the people concerned who matter. If your hearts are in tune, then you can make it happen.'

If your hearts are in tune, Carrie mused later as she was driven home by Bert, Robert having decided to drive his daughter back to his own home so that she could make friends with Felix.

Aunt Aggie was wrong, age *did* matter, at least to Robert. He might have met the right woman for him, but making him see that would be impossible.

The exam for the Croxton Prize proved far easier than Carrie had thought. Hardly a walkover, but, thanks to extra tuition from Robert and from her uncle, most of the questions presented no difficulty to her, and she was cautiously pleased with her efforts, and she prepared for the hospital ball the following day in an optimistic mood.

Judy was wearing a delicately patterned gown of lavender and lemon flowers on a white background, but for herself it was the flame dress. She didn't wear the pearls, after all, and had offered them on loan to Judy, who had hesitated before refusing.

'No, I ought not to, Carrie, but thanks, anyway.' Judy snapped her gold bracelet into place. 'I wonder if he'll bring me flowers? This dress is a bit "busy" and I wouldn't want a corsage, really. Still, he looks the romantic type, doesn't he?'

'I don't think surgeons *are* romantic,' Carrie chimed in, then stood back to admire herself in the mirror in Judy's room. 'Shall I put my hair up or leave it?' She tugged a strand of the rich, foxy hair, and began to brush it.

'Mm? Oh, leave it down, Carrie. It's too sophisticated for you swept up into a bun. Time enough for that when you're past thirty,' Judy said firmly.

Carrie pulled a face at her in the mirror, and was about to make some comment when the telephone rang.

'Oh, you get it, Carrie, there's a pet! I must just finish my face,' Judy called, and Carrie lifted her skirts and walked carefully down the stairs in her high-heeled strappy sandals.

Wondering where their uncle was, Carrie barely had time to repeat their number when an anxious voice broke in, 'Oh, Carrie! It's Ella. Can you come? Daddy's awfully poorly. I don't know what to do, and Great-Aunt Aggie says leave him alone, he'll be fine, but he won't! Can you get a taxi out here?' Ella's voice was lonely and forlorn, and Carrie's heart went out to her.

'Of course I can, but are you sure I can help? What's the matter with him?'

There was a small silence, and Carrie frowned, wondering what was going on. 'Ella? Are you still there? What's the matter with Daddy?'

'I don't know,' Ella said at last. 'He's gone off his food, and just sits around looking yellow.'

'Yellow! Do you mean he's jaundiced?' All sorts of explanations flashed through Carrie's mind. What had given him jaundice? Had he picked up an infection from a patient?

'What's jaundiced? Isn't that yellow skin? He hasn't got a yellow skin, I didn't mean *that*.' Ella's voice was plaintive. 'He's not been himself for ages, and he certainly can't come to your ball. Couldn't you pop in and look at him? You're a nurse, after all!'

'I've just started my second year as a *student* nurse,' Carrie pointed out carefully. 'If he's ill, he needs a doctor. Shall I send Uncle Charles? He'll know what to do and he——'

At the other end of the telephone there was the sound of heart-rending sobs, and Carrie gave in. 'All right, I'll get a taxi. Where are you? At your own home or Aunt Aggie's?'

'At home. Appledore,' Ella gulped. 'Please come soon,

Carrie.' Then the line went dead and Carrie was left holding the receiver. She was just replacing it, her mind in a whirl, when Judy appeared on the landing.

'What's the matter? Has something dreadful happened?'

'I'm not sure,' Carrie said slowly. 'That was Ella. She said Robert's ill. She mentioned jaundice but I don't——'

'Jaundice?' Judy shrieked. 'Why did he have to get that on the night of the ball? It's just too bad, on top of everything else,' she moaned, coming down towards Carrie. 'I suppose he needs tender loving care and you're going to give it?'

'I can hardly *not* go,' Carrie said reasonably. 'Ella wants me to get a taxi there—you wouldn't give me a lift, I suppose?' Judy had her own car and it wouldn't take all that long.

Judy shook her head. 'You're right, I wouldn't! I'm all ready for the ball; how can I drive out into the back of beyond? Anyway——' She seemed about to say more, then stopped abruptly. 'You go, Carrie. Give him my love and tell him I'll dance with him another time.'

'But if you love him of course you want to be with him!' Carrie exclaimed, unable to understand her sister's attitude. 'You do love him, don't you?'

'Yes,' Judy conceded. 'He's very good-looking. Rich and personable. But—oh, he'll understand. I think him rather a bore sometimes. All he talks about when we're out is a certain Student Nurse West! Almost as if——' She stopped again, while Carrie's heart began to beat faster. 'Hurry up and nurse him back to health, Carrie, then perhaps he'll be in time for the end of the ball,' Judy finished, disappearing back into her room.

Sighing at her sister's stupidity, Carrie went in search of her uncle, who agreed straight away to drive her to Appledore. 'That's unusual for Robert. Being ill, I mean. Never anything wrong with the man. We surgeons have to be a tough bunch, you know. Still. . .' He peered at

Carrie as if seeing her for the first time. 'You're looking very fetching, but that's hardly the ensemble to wear if you're going to do a spot of nursing. Want to change?'

'No, I—no, I won't stop to change. I'll just get my coat.' Carrie flew up the stairs and was ready to leave in a few minutes. She ought to change, of course, but she did so want Robert to see her in her finery. Perhaps he might feel better if he saw her, or he might tease her about redheads not wearing red dresses. It would divert his attention, anyway.

All through the journey she was rehearsing to herself what she would say. Despite Ella's anguished call, she didn't think Robert was at death's door. Perhaps he had lost a patient; that would be enough to put him in a blue mood for weeks to come. Yes, that must be it. 'Oh, please don't let him be *really* ill,' she murmured to herself, willing her uncle to drive more quickly. It wasn't as if they had to drive out to Merehurst, for Appledore was only at the other end of town, on the outskirts, but it seemed a very long way.

Her agitated ringing on the doorbell was answered after a long interval by Ella, who peered out at them. 'You've been ages, Carrie! Hello, Uncle Charles. Come into the kitchen and I'll make you a nice hot drink. Daddy's in the study—with Felix,' she added, taking Carrie's astonished uncle by the hand and leading him away, leaving Carrie to close the front door and find her way to Robert's study, her mind numb.

Robert swung round as Carrie entered without knocking, her eyes wide with apprehension. He was sitting at his desk, and Felix was lapping at a saucer near Robert's feet.

'What on earth are *you* doing here?' he demanded, his tone causing the cat to look up in surprise.

'I thought you were ill,' Carrie faltered, advancing into the room, the filmy dress drifting about her. 'Uncle Charles brought me. Ella said you had jaundice. At least I thought she said that.'

'Jaundice!' Robert echoed, catching her by the arms and pulling her to him. 'Jaundice? I'm sure she said nothing of the kind! I doubt if she knows what the word means.' He began to stroke her cheek, then pinched her chin between thumb and forefinger. 'You're looking swell tonight, Carrie, a real belle of the ball.'

'No, that's Judy,' Carrie said, still perplexed. 'Wait until you see her. She's wearing a——'

'You aren't a reporter describing a royal fashion parade, Nurse West,' he said grimly, releasing her. 'I do not want to know what your beautiful, elegant but cold-blooded sister is wearing. Is that clear?'

'Yes, sir,' Carrie said meekly, causing him to lift an eyebrow.

'Not going to call me a chauvinistic whatsit? Or a rich rentier?'

'If you're dying of some mysterious yellow disease, I ought to be kind to you,' she said primly, seating herself behind his desk. 'This is a comfy chair, sir.'

'I'm glad you approve, Nurse West. Tell me, how did the Croxton go?'

Carrie's eyes danced, and she proceeded to tell him, question by question. 'And the final question was on the emotional aspects of gynae ops!' she whooped.

He smiled grimly. 'I'm glad. You'll go far, Carrie. One day I shall find your name among the list of chief nursing officers.'

Carrie got up, then laid her hand against his cheek. She had to stand on tiptoe to do so, and brushed against the cat. 'Sorry, Felix,' she murmured. 'I don't want to be a chief nursing officer, I want to—to belong to a consultant surgeon named Robert Sheraton,' she said, greatly daring. If she had learned one thing from her sister, it was that sometimes love—and men—needed a helping hand. She couldn't afford to wait until Robert realised how grown-up she was, she had to show him—now. Still on tiptoe, she gently brushed her lips against his, but was disconcerted to hear him chuckle.

Laughter glinted in Robert's eyes, 'Nurse West, I do believe you're flirting with me! You must have been taking lessons from your sister. Here, let me show you how it's done.'

This he proceeded to do, and he did it so well that Carrie was left breathless. They clung together, two lonely people who had at last found each other.

'You aren't really ill, are you?' she whispered, eyes uncertain as she gazed at him. 'I couldn't bear it if you were!'

'I rather think Ella has a lot to answer for.' Tenderly he smiled down at Carrie, then kissed the tip of her little nose. 'She told me only this morning that it was time she had a mother, and she suggested you for the part. I—a love like Mireille and I had comes only once in a lifetime, my dear,' he went on, holding her a little apart from him. 'It was an all-consuming passion, destined to burn itself out very quickly. But it *was* love, we did love each other and, despite what anyone might say, we would have stayed together. I want you to understand that. If I don't talk about Mireille, it's because I loved her so, and that remains a private memory, not to be shared.'

Carrie swallowed. 'I understand, Robert, really. But perhaps we might have a good relationship, too?'

'A good relationship? That sounds rather tame!' He tilted her chin, forcing her to meet his dark gaze. 'Do you think you could love me just a little, if you tried?'

'I've always loved you! I thought you knew that. I think I have ever since you were my Good Samaritan. Whatever happened to that woman? The one with the laser eyes?'

'Laser eyes?'

'Hm, she was in the car with you last December when you rescued Phil Mackie and me.'

'Oh, that one! Good lord, I can't remember,' he admitted. 'No, that isn't true, her name was Alison—

but that's in the past, Carrie, *my* past. You haven't had time for much past, have you?'

Carrie shook her head, and Robert caught one of the gleaming strands of bright hair and wrapped it gently around his finger, pulling her towards him again. 'Do you think you could bear to have Ella as a stepdaughter? She's been spoiled, she's temperamental, she's——'

'She's adorable,' Carrie said firmly, beaming at him. 'Were you offering marriage, then, sir?'

'Why, yes, I do believe I was, Nurse. No, it isn't an offer, it's an order. I order you to obey me without question in the future, Mrs Sheraton. Will you do that?'

'No, absolutely not, sir,' she murmured, and they laughed together, the soft, warming laughter of lovers. 'What about Sister Whitworth?' she murmured drowsily, her eyes tightly closed.

'She's an old friend, and if you're going to question me about *all* the women I know I shall have to take steps, Nurse!'

'Sorry.' Carrie was unrepentant. 'Kiss me again, please, sir.'

'As I'm called "Caroline's Conquest", I suppose I shall have to obey,' he acknowledged. Then their lips met and there was no more time for talking. Carrie felt Felix rub against her leg then miaow for another dish of milk. Even he had found a home and a family.

— *MEDICAL* ❤ *ROMANCE* —

The books for enjoyment this month are:

THE SINGAPORE AFFAIR Kathleen Farrell
CAROLINE'S CONQUEST Hazel Fisher
A PLACE OF REFUGE Margaret Holt
THAT SPECIAL JOY Betty Beaty

❤ ❤ ❤ ❤ ❤

Treats in store!

Watch next month for the following absorbing stories:

MORE THAN TIME Caroline Anderson
LOVING QUEST Frances Crowne
CLOSER TO A STRANGER Lilian Darcy
DIAMONDS FROM DR DALY Angela Devine